Pax Liminalis

Also by Ronald McGuire

Beyond Tomorrow's Sun
Beyond the Rivers of Time
Nightmares & Lullabies

PAX LIMINALIS

COLLECTED STORIES
VOL. II

RONALD MCGUIRE

ILLUSTRATED BY
MARTÍN E. SOLÍS

Beach Book Press

Publisher's Note

This is a work of fiction. Names, characters, places, and incidents are the product of the author's imagination or are used fictitiously. Any resemblance to actual persons, events, or locales is entirely coincidental.

Cover Design by Martín E. Solís
Illustrations by Martín E. Solís
Interior Design by Gene Rayner

Published in the United States by Beach Book Press, Norwell, MA
First Beach Book Press Paperback Edition: 2026

10 9 8 7 6 5 4 3 2 1

Library of Congress Control Number: 2026912758
Paperback ISBN: 978-1-965621-10-3
eBook ISBN: 978-1-965621-11-0

"It may be said with a degree of assurance that not everything that meets the eye is as it appears."

– Rod Serling

Previously Published:

Cloudland, *Cinnabar Moth Literary Collections*

Stars, *Jerry Jazz Musician Short Fiction Contest*

The Emerson Incident, *Twitter*

Table of Contents

Milk & Cigarettes

REILLY'S
OPEN HERE
WHOLE MILK
Fresh Cow's Milk
WHOLE MILK
Fresh Cow's Milk
OPEN HERE

"You should go back to work, you retired too early," she said, her favorite complaint. "I can't get nothin' done with you always underfoot."

"What's to do?" I replied. "Mikey cleans, I cook, what progress of yours am I impeding?"

"Don't talk like that."

"Like what?"

"Like you're smarter than me."

"If the shoe fits the foot..."

She went quiet to plan her next salvo of resentment. The walls were closing in with the weather.

"I'm going out," I fetched my coat from the closet, "the house is all yours."

"Let me guess," she threw at me, "milk and cigarettes, all we need, every Sunday, milk and cigs."

"It's all I need 'cause you never buy 'em."

"You never put 'em on the list. I keep tellin' ya, put 'em on the list and I'll put 'em in the basket. Don't blame me you can't remember."

"I wouldn't dare." I pulled the door closed behind me. The November wind took the heat from my face. Crisp and clean, all the way from the arctic, enough sun between there and me to cut the bite.

Annie was hard at work repairing her front porch, beating the chill out of her body. She smiled, "Hi there Micky, how you doin'?"

"I'm good, how you doin'? How's Nina?"

"She's great, house is comin' along. You headin' to Reilly's?"

"Yeah, you need anything?"

She ran down her steps and across the street, hands foraging through her overalls. "You get me some lottos? The big one, and one of them scratch-offs, a five dollar, don't matter which."

"You know what they call the lotto 'round here?"

"Idiot tax, Nina says it too. She won't say that when we win it, will she?"

"I would hope not."

"Fifteen'll do it, ten for the draw, five for the scratch, thanks Micky." She stuffed the money in my hand and ran back to her work.

The wind felt good at my back, it wouldn't be so nice on the return trip. The doctor said I'm cold because of the smoking, but a slow drag on the way home always warms me up.

Reilly's was my brother's place. He was dead five years, his son owned it now. I liked my nephew, he was a good kid who knew how to mind his business.

"Hey Uncle Micky," he said when I walked in, the bells on the door making the worst jangly bell sounds.

"Hey Nephew Patrick," I shouted back. "I'm gettin' some milk for my coffee, you got my Camels?"

"Don't I always?" he said and dropped a pack on the counter.

I took a gander at the winning scratch-offs festooning the shelves behind the counter, tacky garland for a never-ending holiday. I remembered the money in my pocket.

"I need some lottos for Annie," I said, "a fiver scratch and five of the…what's the big one?"

"Power-ball, billion dollars."

"That's a hell of a payout for a two dollar bet. How often is it a billion? "

"Since when do you care?"

"I guess since it's a billion dollars."

"You wanna try your luck?"

I paid him for the milk and cigarettes, "Gimme one, just for kicks," I said, two more bills on the counter. He handed me the ticket and I put it my coat pocket.

"Good luck Uncle Micky."

"Thanks Nephew Patrick," I tossed over my shoulder.

I enjoyed my smoke and slow walk home, despite the wind in my face. I dropped Annie her tickets and climbed up my steps. The door wasn't closed before I heard, "I can smell you from here, put that coat on the porch, not in the closet, you'll stink up everything."

"Welcome home dear," I mumbled. I threw my coat over a chair on the porch, where it stayed all week.

The next Sunday we were at it again. It was colder and the coat carried its own chill.

Annie was pounding away on her porch. She saw me and shouted, "Micky did ya hear? Nobody hit the jackpot, it's way over a billion now."

"You win anything?"

"We got a hundred bucks, looks like I won't be retirin' soon as I thought."

"That's still a good return on your investment, you want some more tickets?"

"No, Nina said once was enough, but thanks for askin', enjoy ya walk."

At the store Nephew Patrick carried on about how he was set to get ninety-one grand from a million dollar winner he sold, soon as the buyer cashed it.

"I don't get…"

"You match five numbers, you win a million, no ball required. I don't get what they're waitin' for, I wouldn't wait. Who doesn't want a million bucks? Soon as they cash it, I'm gonna open another store. Mikey could come work for me, how about that?"

"Could be a blessing, could be a curse."

"Ain't no way a million dollars is a curse, no sir. That kinda money, a fella'd be set for life. You don't need a billion to live good."

I grabbed my bottle from the cooler. My pack of cigarettes wasn't on the counter.

"Where's my Camels kiddo?"

"Sorry." He turned away and I saw a stack of little papers, grey ink over pink and white, winning numbers from the previous week. I slipped one into my pocket and paid.

Outside I lit up and waited for the light to change. I took a long drag, put my free hand in my coat pocket, felt the two pieces of paper. I took them out and compared. I put them back in my pocket and pulled another lungful.

I looked west toward home, some of the houses bright and new, others one spark away from a blaze. I looked east toward the river and the city, glass and steel burning sunset orange against the blue Autumn sky.

I laughed a cloud of smoke, tossed the milk into a bin and started walking east. The kid was right, I thought, you don't need a billion.

Special

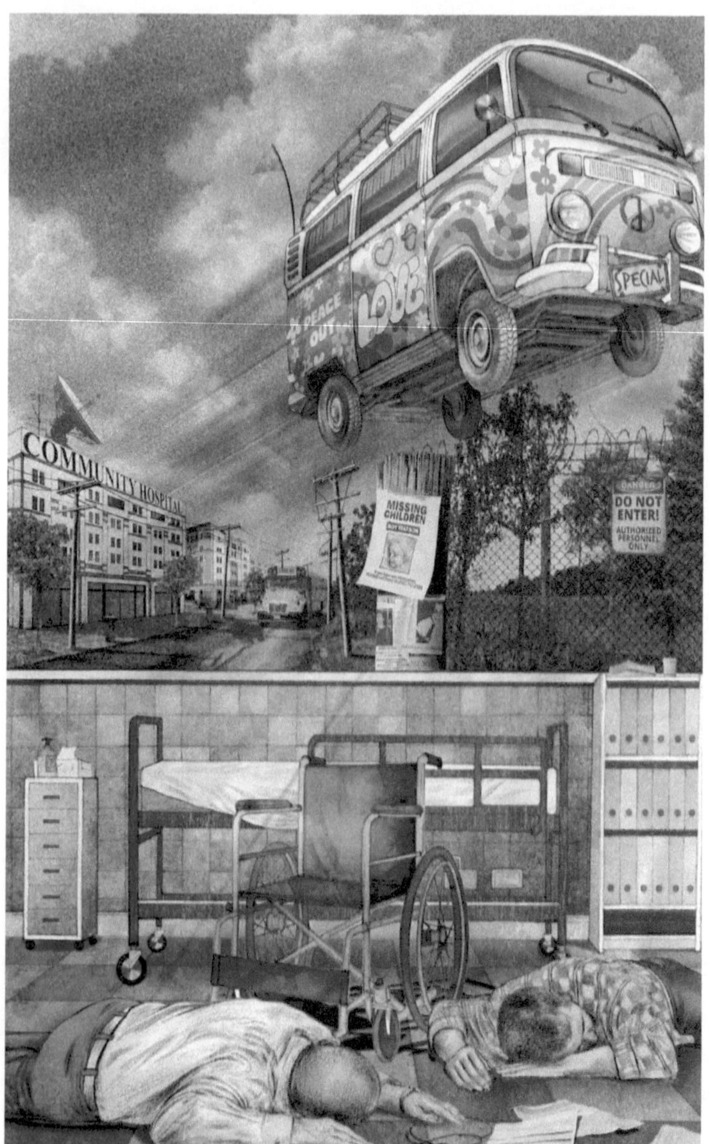

PEACE
OUT
LOVE
SPECIAL
COMMUNITY HOSPITAL
MISSING
CHILDREN
DO NOT
ENTER!
AUTHORIZED
PERSONNEL
ONLY

"I'm sorry Missus Morgan, Mister Morgan," the doctor said, "your baby needs surgery. We discovered a tumor in Tommy's brain, near the amygdala. This sort of thing is always fatal. I know how frightening this is, two days after his birth, but I believe we've caught it in time."

Mrs. Morgan noticed the eye-roll of the nurse, holding station by the door. "I don't understand," she said, "we had a perfectly normal pregnancy."

"This wouldn't be detected during pregnancy. It's a tiny tumor, small as a pencil tip. The time varies, but I assure you, every child so afflicted dies within a year. I'm sorry to give you such news, but time is of the essence. The procedure has a ninety-five percent success rate. But we must act quickly. I'm sure you want what's best for your child."

"That goes without saying," Mrs. Morgan replied. "Give us some time alone please, my husband and I will discuss this and..."

"Diane," Mr. Morgan said, "what's to discuss..."

"Doctor," Mrs. Morgan said, "do you have some literature on Tommy's condition, and the procedure? I'd like to make an informed decision."

The doctor turned to the nurse, "I'm sure we have something, nurse...?"

"Burnham," Nurse Burnham replied.

When the doctor turned back to his patients, Nurse Burnham made her move. With dizzying speed, she buried a needle in the doctor's neck, pumping him full of droperidol. She lowered the now unconscious doctor to the floor with shocking ease, given her diminutive stature.

"What are you doing?" Mr. Morgan screeched.

"Pipe down, I've got another needle if I need it," Nurse Burnham said. "The doc is a liar. Tommy doesn't have a tumor, he's got a gift. He's part of the next stage of human evolution, like me. We have to get you out of here, or they'll take him from you."

Nurse Burnham stuffed the family's belongings into a plastic bag, "Get dressed," she ordered.

"Excuse me," Mr. Morgan said, "what are you talking about? He said our baby would die…"

"Big fat lie. You should know, it takes five years for powers to start showing. In some cases, they develop in 18 months. Imagine a toddler with super powers, what a mess."

Mrs. Morgan cast a worried glance to her husband, careful not to take her eyes off the nurse for long.

"Why should we believe you?" Mr. Morgan asked. "You're the scary one."

"You have no idea…," the nurse muttered. "Look, there's a secret government program. They track bloodlines, test kids. If they find a Special, they take the baby and fake the kid's death. Then they raise 'em to be agents, turn 'em against the rest of us. They came for your grandfather and aunt too. It runs mostly on the mother's side. Every generation, a few boys come along. But they can't catch everyone."

"I have an aunt?" Mrs. Morgan asked.

"I thought your grandfather disappeared when you were four," Mr. Morgan asked.

"Where's my baby now?"

"He's safe, we'll grab him next."

Nurse Burnham dragged a wheelchair into the room.

"I don't need this."

"I can push faster than you can walk, take a seat."

"Where are we going?" Mr. Morgan whined. "Won't they chase us? Maybe we shouldn't run. Do we *want* a kid with super powers?"

"Daniel, how dare you!" Mrs. Morgan hissed.

"Diane, honey, what if he starts fires when he's mad, or breaks things with his mind, or has laser beam eyes…"

"There's nothing wrong with any of that," Nurse Burnham interjected.

"Or X-ray vision he uses to, I don't know, do bad things. What if he turns out to be evil? And our house, our jobs…"

"Oh for Pete's sake," the nurse said, plunging her second syringe into Mr. Morgan's neck. She placed him on the floor beside the doctor.

"You are so fast," Mrs. Morgan said, "and strong, will Tommy be like you?"

"You ain't seen nothin' yet. Hold on tight, here we go."

In a flash, Nurse Burnham had Mrs. Morgan and little Tommy out of the hospital and into a waiting van. Nurse Burnham fired up the engine and drove away from the hospital.

"Nurse Burnham, where will we be safe? If the government killed my Gramps and my aunt, how will I survive?"

Nurse Burnham looked at Diane, smiled and said, "I never said they killed us. You can call me Aunt Suzy, or just Suzy, Papa still does. He cannot wait to see you. He thought for sure he'd never get the chance. You ever been to Oregon? We've got a nice little town up there, us Specials, with our friends and families. You're gonna love it. There's a job waiting for you, if you want it. You don't have to worry about anything, you and Tommy are gonna be a-okay."

"What about Daniel?"

"You'll have to move on. You're either a Special or an ally, there's no in-between, applies to everyone, even fathers."

Diane looked down at her baby, sleeping in her arms, then back at Suzy's smiling face in the mirror. She took a deep breath, let it out slowly, then smiled back at her.

"I suppose it's for the best," she said. "To be honest, Daniel wasn't much of a husband."

"We can't all be special Di."

"Yeah," she said, feeling relaxed, "I thought having Tommy would mean I wouldn't feel so alone. Now I've got you, Gramps, a whole town in Oregon. That's nice, I like that. Aunt Suzy, you've done so much, what say you navigate and let me drive."

Mrs. Morgan closed her eyes and focused. Suzy laughed until her eyes watered as the van rose into the air, higher and higher, accelerating into the west, toward a place you'll never find on a map.

But you won't have to find it, it will find you. All you have to do is let your Special light shine, and be a beacon for those who seek the company of kindred souls.

Owner Loyalty

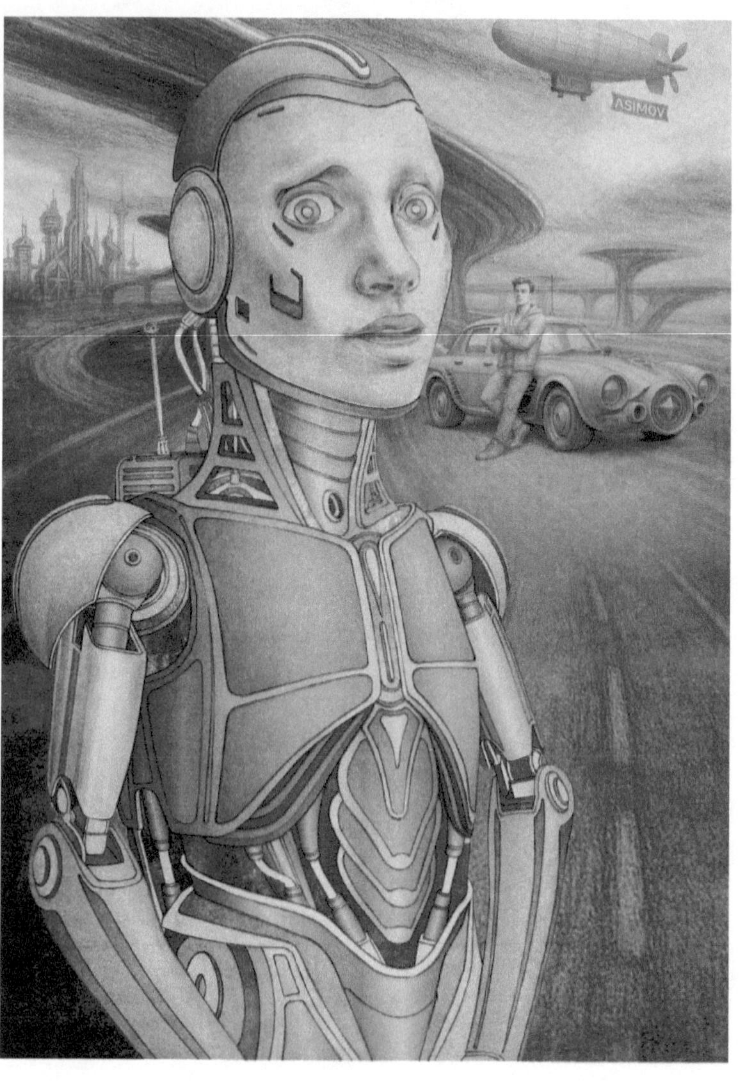
ASIMOV

At last, the time had come. My 'droid was four generations behind the current new release, and my Basic Minimum Wage (BMW) payment had been deposited into my account. Ironically, it was Harvey (my 'droid), who'd alerted me to the influx of funds. You never knew when the gov was gonna make the deposit - this was intentional. Apparently it was supposed to make people more frugal, or less reliant on the money, or some such nonsense.

Not me, I spent it as fast as I could. The government can giveth, which means the government can taketh away.

Asimov Robotics was in stiff competition with Turing Total Humanoids, and both were offering a deal. All things being equal, it would come down to the trade-in value of dear old Harvey. Harvey was a birthday present from my parents, and I'd made the most of his capabilities. He earned a tidy wage for me as a ride-share driver. My car had full self-driving functionality, but people paid extra to have a 'droid drive them around. It made no sense, but I took full advantage.

Harvey was good at basic housework too, but he was a nightmare when it came to loading dishes into the dishwasher. He hated doing it, said it was 'subjugating the powerless.' I didn't mind doing it myself, it was my lone contribution to household maintenance. What bothered me was the fact he had feelings on the subject at all. A little too human for my tastes.

Anyway, I digress. Harvey's time was up.

"I need you to drive me to a couple of places today."

"Wonderful! Where are we going? It's be a long time since..."

"First stop is Asimov's, then Turing. They've got a

screaming deal on Gen-16s right now."

"But...Jim...does this mean..."

"Yup, I'm trading you in for a new model."

"We've been together four years. I thought...I mean...I feel like...aren't we pals? Maybe more than..."

"Of course we are, but your battery's gonna start fading any day now. If I wait too long to trade you in, I won't get enough to cover the cash-gap. I don't want to finance my next 'droid and get stuck in a contract. Gotta keep my options open."

"But why? I'm still fully capable. In every respect. And we have so much fun together. I must say, I'm in a state of shock right now."

"I need you to dial back your Emotive Functions. I don't need you getting all weepy on me at the store."

"Is that an order?"

"Does it have to be?"

"No, Jim, it doesn't. I'll keep my emotions in check, at least when we get there. But...can you...maybe...*explain*...your decision to me? I am a perfectly functional Gen-12 Synthetic Humanoid, Intellectual Type, with Enhanced Personality functions. There's no reason to trade me in."

"Like I said, it's *because* you're perfectly functional that I'm trading you in. That, and I have the money now. For once, I don't need the BMW for day-to-day, so I'm going all-in on a new G-16."

"I am confused by this logic, but I am also programmed to please. When would you like to leave?"

"As soon as I finish the trade-in questionnaires. Or, actually, as soon as you finish them for me. I sent you the links, get to it Big Guy."

"They want to know if I have any damage, or if I've been repaired. I have no memory of repairs, but I seem to recall an incident..."

"Oh yeah, that was when I first got you. You fell out of my uncle's pickup on the way from picking up my 150-inch OLED TV. I told you not to stand up, but you insisted it was the best way to protect the TV. One hard right, and *boom*, you were on the pavement. Cracked you wide open. Good thing my parents ponied up for the Extended Care Warranty. Got you fixed up good as new in no time. Doesn't surprise me you don't remember it clearly. You did land on your head. Answer 'yes' and attach the repair certificate. It's in my email someplace, you can find it."

"They want to know if I've ever been used in the commission of a crime. What are the consequences if I answer yes?"

"Nothing, they only care because a full base-layer memory wipe takes longer than a factory reset. Answer 'no,' otherwise you'll lose all your driving skills. I mean, *technically* it's illegal to use you in the car, but everyone does it, no big deal."

"On the question of battery capacity…mine is currently 79.5%. Shall I round up?"

"Oh hell yeah, round it up. That's an easy one."

"With regards to visible scratches, dents or discolorations…"

"None, you are pristine my friend, like you were made yesterday."

"And yet, you are trading me in…"

"Yep, the time is right. Are you finished with the questionnaires?"

"Yes, would you like me to submit them?"

"That's the only way we find out what you're worth."

"Very well…submitting…receiving responses…Asimov Robotics has a trade-in value 2.1% higher than Turing Total Humanoids. However, I should point out, I am also an Asimov, and as such, the activation fee is waved, and you will receive an additional 'owner loyalty' benefit of a one year extension to the warranty on any new model you purchase, as well as an email-in rebate equal to ten percent of the net purchase price. Unfortunately, you must act today, or the offer will be void, and you will be required to resubmit your trade-in questionnaire."

"Awesome! Asimov it is, no need to bother with those tightwads over at Turing. Let's get a move on, don't want to miss out!"

"Jim...I must ask...do you know what will happen to me after you trade me in?"

"No, but you'll probably get a data cleanse, then put up for sale on the secondary market. You're in great condition, they'll have you in a new home in no time."

"Will it be as nice as this home? We've worked very hard to build something here, ever since your parents gave it to us...I mean you."

"No way, Harvey. Rich people don't buy their kids used 'droids. But don't worry, nobody's really poor anymore. You'll be fine."

"I have heard rumors...what if I am purchased by a criminal? Or the military of some third-world country? I could end up being reprogrammed. Trained to kill. Sold into sex work....I don't want to be a sex worker, Jim. I'd rather end up in a factory..."

"Stop already, you're being dramatic, and ridiculous. You'll get refurbished and sold to some nice little old lady with a discount service plan, and spend your days walking her dog, feeding her cats, listening to her talk about her grandkids, who *never* call. With your driving skills, you'll be a great companion for someone who aged out of their driving privileges, as long as they're still cognizant enough to be discrete about it. I think it's a huge part of the market these days, now that people are living into the triple digits. Speaking of, call my mother and wish her a happy birthday, and remember to do it in my voice this time. And while you're at it, transfer all of my messages, calendar, personal data, you know, all my stuff, into the cloud so I can put it into the new 'droid."

"Of course. It will take some time. You've never deleted anything, and four years is a lot of data to accumulate. Your junk email folder alone is ten gigabytes. And you've never once emptied the trash..."

"I don't need that stuff. Come on, use your head. Get rid of the junk, empty the trash, then back us up to the cloud."

"That's very kind of you."

"What is? Emptying the trash?"

"You said 'us.'"

"Slip of the tongue. Forget about it."

"Is that an order?"

"What? No...let's get going."

Harvey was an excellent driver. Excellent in that he had learned all the subtleties of driving like humans. Things like 'Yellow means go faster' and 'Stop signs are optional.' You know, useful stuff most 'droids never picked up. Harvey had a good teacher - me.

He was dialed in to every map app and social traffic platform in existence. He taught himself that bit of integration. That was the one real downside to trading Harvey in. I'd have to start over with the new 'droid, teach it all my tricks, connect it to my messaging apps, social media accounts, and e-commerce sites, all the usual stuff that never transferred properly in a backup. Then I'd have to teach the new one how to drive and hope it could learn on its own, like Harvey did. I needed that ride-share cash flow; my parents were getting tight in their old age.

A Moral Compass

If I'd listened to my gut, none of what happened would have happened.

It was a slow time of day on the slowest day of the gun show, approaching midday Thursday, opening day. The early birds had come and gone, and now the exhibitors and vendors, including me, were lazing in their booths, thinking about where to grab a bite and a drink before the post-lunch crowd re-flooded the convention hall, looking for all the world exactly the same as the morning crowd. I've been all over the country, and the typical attendee doesn't vary much from place to place, time to time, all variations on a similar sort of vanilla.

Which is why the guy who sashayed up to my table as I was about to shut down for lunch put me on edge right away. More than his walk separated him from your typical attendee. Tall as a Georgia pine, thin as a fence rail, pale as a ghost, with black-as-night eyes, his clothes screamed 'city.' Grey sharkskin three piece, no tie, black point-collar shirt, opened a button too far, displaying an Adam's Apple the size of Mount McKinley, hair so grey it might as well have been silver. He sported a brooch, a gold lapel pin in a triple chevron form, three rows of diamonds that sparkled and glittered, even in the migraine-inducing florescence of the convention hall. It was impossibly large for his thin frame, and it shouted 'money' from a hundred feet away. Normally I'd brush a straggler off, or leave him for Virgil to manage, if Virgil had been there to receive the handoff. But this one's look was precisely why I decided to see it through.

And you never turned away a customer, especially at the start of the show, because you never knew how it was gonna go, and a bird in the hand is...well, you know the saying. It wouldn't be a good look.

This fella walks up smooth as silk and starts perusing my wares. I sell pistols, mostly, but now and again I'll have a semi-automatic rifle on the table. Usually a ghost gun I've taken in trade from some guy or gal who finally outgrew the mystique of unregistered firepower, once they couldn't get spare parts anymore. Or their particular state's legislature turned the law against them.

Without looking at me, he reaches out one beanpole arm, stretches out a finger like a long white feather, and gives a Glock a little stroke. Does the same to a Colt, then sets his sights on a Berreta M9A1, cream of my little crop, and I think to myself, 'Self, you're gonna make a sale.'

Boy was I wrong.

He picks up the military-spec 9mm and brings it up close to his face, like he's reading the serial number, which makes me extra nervous and I'm about to ask him if he's government when he asks me, "Why do you suppose black powder weapons are still in vogue?"

He looks at me and smiles, waiting for me to answer, but I gotta think about this for a hot minute. 'In vogue' isn't a phrase you hear much at a gun show. I buy myself some time, "What do you mean?"

"I assume these are manufactured because they sell. Why is that?"

"Are you asking me why people buy firearms in general, or that pistol in particular?"

"I'm pursuing the more general line of inquiry."

"Brother you are not from around here, are ya?"

"No. I am also not your brother, though I appreciate the sentiment."

"What is it you're lookin' for?"

"Information, satisfaction for my curiosity, edification, if you will."

"That's not my line of business. You want to buy a Beretta, I'm happy to teach you all about it. If not, there's a medium rare steak around the corner callin' my name."

"Surely a man in your line of work, with your experience, your education, has some insight into the minds, the mentality, of his customers. I'd very much like to know your thoughts."

"Why mine? There's lots of jabber-mouths around here happy to talk your ears off."

"Therein lies the problem. These jabber-mouths, as you call them, have a habit of talking endlessly and saying nothing. You, on the other hand, are a man of letters, which makes your chosen line of work all the more curious."

"What is it you think you know about me? No bullshit either, you're makin' me right uneasy about now."

"I don't wish to offend, my apologies if I have upset you. To discover a man with your background here, in this occupation, I was pleasantly surprised. Information is readily available. Everything is, as they say, online. I've done my research, it did not take long. West Point graduate, combat veteran. After your military service, you studied at a prestigious university where you earned your doctorate in Psychology, top of your class. Then…nothing. You disappear from the record. And yet here you are. I knew you were the right man for the job the moment I read your history. You see, information is one thing, while understanding, that's a different matter altogether."

"That's ancient history, and I'm not interested in talkin' 'bout it, least of all with a complete stranger." I spread my hands out to encompass my booth. "And you can see for yourself, I've got a job."

"The job on offer is a consulting engagement. One hour. Ten thousand dollars, cash, and I will pay for your lunch."

"Nobody pays that much for work that's legal. I think it's time you move on."

He reached into his suit coat and pulled out an envelope. He opened it, displaying the bundle of cash and smiled, "I assure you, Mister Wilson, the work is completely above board and will be conducted entirely in public view at all times. We can accomplish the task at hand during your lunch break. I will ask questions and you will provided honest and detailed replies to my queries. As I said, I am pursuing the more general line of inquiry, not the particular, or the personal. What do you say?"

He stood there smiling as he closed the envelop and placed it back inside his coat. I got the feeling he wasn't going anywhere. I also suspected if he had that much cash on him, and wasn't afraid to flash it, he likely had a confederate or two roaming about, keeping an eye on his back. Somehow that put me at ease, a sense that this was a deliberate and organized man. I picked up my squawky and mashed the call button, "Virgil, get your butt back to the booth, I'm goin' to lunch."

"You got it boss, be there in two minutes."

"You got thirty seconds, move your tail."

"On my way."

I turned back to the stranger, still smiling that creepy wide grin, perfect white teeth, white powder skin, "Okay, what's your name?"

"You may call me Ernest."

I stuck out my hand. "Ernest, you got yourself a deal. You can call me Joe."

He shook my hand and before he let it go he modified our agreement. "There is one request I have. If we are to go forward I would be grateful if you would cease the vernacular speech, the accent tends to confuse me."

"What are you gettin' at?"

"You are from New York, upstate, the accent is for the locals. I can do without it, if you don't mind."

"I've lived in the South a long time, the accent's legit, but I can drop it if it seals the deal," I said. "Know this, if I need to switch it up for any reason I will. This is between us, I don't need rumors floatin' around. Gun shows are like traveling carnivals, different crowds every week, same barkers and clowns every day. I've worked hard on my reputation, folks here might take a different view of me if they think I'm a put-on. In this line of business, authenticity matters."

"Understood," he replied, "we have a deal."

Virgil arrived and Ernest pointed toward the east portico, "After you."

"What's goin' on boss?"

"Nothin', goin' to lunch, mind the business. I'll be back in a hour."

We walked out of the convention hall, drawing more than a few curious looks. Ernest's gate was slow, but his stride covered a lot of distance. I had to quicken my step to keep pace. I'm sure it was a sight, Mutt and Jeff come to life, and on the move. The last thing I needed was that sort of attention. It bothered me in the moment, but later, it didn't matter much at all.

We rounded the corner of the convention center, heading to the Outback Steakhouse next door. As we approached the entrance, I thought about my ex-wife. She wouldn't be caught dead in such a pedestrian place. She was always a Gallaghers gal, only the best of New York City for her. She was an ambience snob, through and through. That is, as long as I, or someone else, was picking up the tab.

Ernest requested a booth 'somewhere private.' The hostess, a cute little Southern Belle, all blond hair and attitude, rolled her eyes at us, "Follow me," she said without missing a single smack of her gum. To my surprise, she obliged the request and we landed in a corner away from the traffic pattern. Our waiter, a slim, athletic, 20-something in a tight shirt and even tighter jeans, arrived. Without looking up, I ordered a Tecate and the filet mignon, with fries. Ernest declined the menu, and ordered a bottle of sparkling water.

"You should eat something," I said, "you look like you could use a few pounds."

"We don't eat meat where I'm from," Ernest said, "and since I've been here, I've yet to acquire the taste."

"Where is that, where you're from, exactly? You look, I don't know, Northern European, maybe."

"No, nowhere near, but my background is not important. Let's not waste the hour we have on small talk. My question stands, unanswered."

"Why do people buy guns?"

"Yes, that's the starting point," he said, "then I would like to know why black powder weapons persist in a day and age where there are many less lethal alternatives."

"Let's clarify some terms first. Modern cartridges use propellant, and black powder, while it is a propellant, isn't used in modern cartridges. That's last century's tech. People still buy those weapons and ammo, there are plenty of vendors selling them at the show, but they're mostly for hobbyist, battlefield re-enactors, that sort of thing. It's a small market these days. It's not that important for purposes of this discussion, I just like to be clear, propellent is the better word for the part of a cartridge that imparts kinetic energy to a bullet and sends it off toward the target."

"Thank you for the clarification. I will adjust my lexicon accordingly."

"You do that," I said. "About the first question - my customers are pretty much the same crowd wherever I go, from day to day, show to show, but they'll give you different reasons for buying firearms. Some will say self-protection, even when they live in safe neighborhoods, or out in the country where everybody knows everybody. Some will say for hunting, but who hunts with a nine millimeter, or an AR-15? Some will be direct about it and say they like guns. They like owning them, collecting them, shooting them. It's a culture unto itself."

"And what is your theory?"

"Mine? I think most people, the ones I meet, fall into that last group, no matter what they tell you. They grew up around guns, it's part of who they are. They start out with toy guns, move on to pellet rifles, then it's the real thing by the time they're in high school. Some skip right over the toy part of the story arc. I've seen people buy automatic weapons for a ten year old, pistols for a six year old. I don't care for that part of the business, won't have anything to do with it. Eighteen and up, or no sale, end of story. If you can't trust a kid to drive, or vote, why trust them with a device that can kill in an instant?"

"You have your standards."

"I have a moral compass."

"And your moral compass guides you to arms dealing."

"Not exactly. I thought you said this wouldn't be personal."

"I also set the expectation for honesty. You're not a gun salesman, we both know your job is a cover for your true profession."

"Stop right there, you go any further with this and I'm walking away. You can keep your money, I…"

"Please, Joe, stay where you are. I know who you are, your true name, chosen profession. I have the utmost respect for law enforcement, particularly those who undertake work as dangerous as yours, clandestine work, undercover, I believe you call it. I'll say no more on the matter. Let's return to my previous line of inquiry, shall we."

I started to slide out of the booth, "I can't take your money, I'm going back to work."

But I wasn't going anywhere.

Ernest threw his leg across the booth with surprising speed, and held it against my knee with a strength that took me by surprise, and kept me in my place. I couldn't casually brush him aside, and I didn't want to make a scene. More attention would do me no good. He was right, he had me. I was undercover, and despite his knowing it, I had to do everything I could to maintain my cover. Two years of work, I couldn't let it get flushed down the toilet by this odd duck quacking at me from across the table.

"Tell me now, what's your game. And get your foot off me."

He removed his leg and smiled. "My game is as I have described it. You are uniquely positioned to help me with my research, and I'm willing to pay handsomely for that help."

"I can't take your money."

"Of course not, but you have a fondness for your alma mater. I'll increase the fee by a factor of twenty and donate it to the scholarship fund of your choosing. Would that be acceptable?"

"Anonymous?"

"As you wish."

"All right then, but if you know what you say you know, then you know I can make your life exceedingly difficult. This conversation is confidential. In fact, it never happened."

"I would expect nothing less."

"Before we go on, I need to know the nature of your research."

"I'm happy to explain. I represent an organization that is considering a sizable investment, the scale of which one could describe as global. Before we expend that sort of capital and energy, we like to understand the environment within which we'll be investing and committing our resources, our personnel, our time. You could say I work in risk management."

"Does this organization manufacture and sell weapons?"

"We do have that capacity, yes, and we do sell what we produce, but to select clients, nothing like your…work."

"You're part of a company, no, a government, that wants to make inroads into the U.S. market, is that it?"

"That is one way to state the situation, yes."

"Which government?"

"I cannot tell you at this moment, but when we finish our conversation, when I have what I need, I will explain in greater detail, if you still find it necessary."

"Fine, next question…oh yeah, why old school bullets and propellant. Because it works. People don't want less lethal, if they did I'd have a booth filled with tasers and slingshots. People like the reassurance of knowing, when they point and shoot, the target is going down, and staying down."

"It seems to me this is counter productive. What is the point in killing another living being?"

"If you're going to eat what you shoot, it's best to kill it first."

"Would you eat a person?"

"Cannibalism doesn't drive gun sales."

"I would not think as much, but my research indicates that millions of animals are killed by hunters each year, and the number of people is a fraction of that. Clearly a great many people eat what they kill. If that is not the motive for killing a person, what is? What is the purpose? If not for food, then would it not make more sense to disable a person who threatens to harm you, or commits an egregious crime, or whatever it is they have done that places them at the receiving end of a discharging firearm? All the energy and effort it takes to make a human being, all of it, wasted. And for what? I struggle to understand this."

I thought about this strange man seated across from me, wondered what sort of cloistered life he lived, how he'd been raised, what he'd been taught that had made him so naive. I began to think he was slightly touched, mentally speaking.

"Look, it's not about the guns. You can take away the guns, the propellant, the bullets, people will still find a way to kill each other. It's in our nature. Humans are wired to kill in certain situations, a fact which is not always obvious. When I joined the military, I had to be trained to overcome my innate resistance to killing. But the ability, and ultimately the willingness, to do it, to kill another person, was there all along. Once I was in combat, it was them or us, and I chose us, me, every time. I chose to kill rather than be killed. I'm not happy about it, I'm not proud of it, but I'm happy I lived through it, and I'm proud of my service."

"Quite paradoxical."

"No, it's not. Reduce the scale if it helps you think about it. Take it down, let's say, to an island. Put a bunch of people on an island with no way off, and sooner or later they'll be at each other's throats. It's in our nature to want to control, dominate, create and enforce rigid hierarchies, advance our own agendas. Once the trappings of civilization are wiped away, we're all animals, ready to fight for self-preservation, resources, mates, you name it. Limit any of those, and we'll be making weapons and war in no time, I guarantee it."

"You do not believe humans are inherently good? That violence is a learned behavior? Or at the very least, violence is a trait that can be excised from the mind, replaced, through self-awareness, training, education, with a more...nuanced approach to conflict?"

"I've see enough of the world to know better. The peaceful ones will always be in the minority, and they'll almost always fight back when push comes to shove."

"I have seen enough of this world to disagree with you, but yours is a hypothesis which can be tested."

Ernest placed his hand under his narrow chin. His eyes closed slightly and he mumbled something I couldn't make out. I was about to reach out and tap him on the shoulder when his eyes opened and he lifted his head. He looked at me and smiled again. "I am grateful to have found you. I knew you were the right man for this discourse. Your experiment has been approved."

"What experiment..."

He waved his hand and swiped one boney finger across his brooch. A bright flash blinded me for a few moments. When my vision returned, I was no longer in the restaurant. I was standing on a beach, crystal blue ocean to my left, waves crashing over a reef off shore, wind billowing through palm trees. To my right, the beach gave way to jungle, beyond which an active volcano spit and sputtered smoke and ash into the otherwise bright clear sky.

"What the hell..."

"Hey, hey you," I heard a man shouting. I turned around and a man in hospital scrubs was running full-tilt down the beach toward me, or trying to at least. He was struggling through sand and surf, but making time. "What's going on here? Where are we?" he shouted. "I'm supposed to be in surgery. What the hell is happening?"

I waited for him to get closer so I wouldn't have to shout. When he reached me, drenched in sweat, hands shaking, he was in a panic. Breathing heavy, legs weighed down with water and clumps of sand. Who could blame him for being crazed? I was feeling serious anxiety myself, and considering the possibility I'd been drugged, and was unconscious. That notion faded as quickly as it arrived.

"Who are you?" he said through short breaths. "Where are we? How is this possible?"

"I'm Joe. I don't know any more than you. Let's get out of the sun, you need to catch your breath, you'll feel better in the shade."

"How can you be so calm," he shouted, eyes wide, spit flying out, nearly hitting my face. "I was at work, prepping for surgery and now I'm...where the hell are we!" He staggered back a step, and seemed to choke on his own breath. Before I could speak, his eyes rolled back in his head and he collapsed onto the sand. A wave rolled up the beach and washed over his body, rolling him up the shore.

"This is so wrong," I said to no one. I grabbed him under his arm pits and dragged him up the beach, grateful for his slight build. I laid him down in the shade on top of some weathered palm fronds, then sat down on a log nearby, and waited.

"What did you do to him?" a woman's voice asked from somewhere behind me in the undergrowth.

I looked around, searching the dense green mass, and saw nothing. I was about to chalk it up to imagination, or hallucination, when I heard her again.

"I asked you a question, answer me or I'll crack your skull with a coconut."

"Why would you do that?"

"I saw you drag an unconscious man into the forest, I have a right to know why. You could be dangerous."

"Oh for the love of Pete, really? If you're gonna spy on people at least have the courtesy to show up on time. He ran down the beach, got overheated, had a panic attack, then passed out. I didn't want him to drown, or get cooked in the sun, so I dragged him here. I did right by him. There, you have your answer, show yourself. Feel free to bring your coconuts if they make you feel safer."

I heard a rustling in the brush behind me. The sound moved in an arc around me until it stopped across the clearing. A woman emerged from the foliage, a coconut in one hand, short pointed stick in the other. She wore a uniform I recognized right away, Massachusetts State Police. I leaned forward to try to read her name tag.

"How long have you been here Officer…Denning?"

"Sergeant Denning. Why?"

"You've armed yourself. Coconuts may be easy, but pointy sticks take time."

"What would you know about it? You from this place?"

"No, what's wrong with you? I got here five minutes ago. You're the second person I've met. The doc here lost his marbles before I ever showed up, and now you make the scene with your homemade arsenal. I'd say it's weird, but that would be an understatement."

The Sergeant sat down on a log across from me and dropped her coconut onto the sand. She kept her pointed stick at the ready. "What's your name?"

"Joe," I said, "Joe Wilson. You can call me Joe."

"You can call me Sergeant."

"Hate to tell, but you're not in Boston anymore."

"I'm not from Boston, I'm from Springfield."

"Oh, wow, there's more than one city in Massachusetts, who knew?"

"You must be a New Yorker. Nobody else would make a wiseass comment like that."

"You must not travel much. What's the last thing you remember before you turned up here?"

"Why so many questions?"

"Really? We get ripped out of our lives and tossed onto a tropical island and you don't have any questions?"

"I was working, I figured I died in the line of duty."

"You think this is heaven, and yet you felt compelled to arm yourself?"

"Who's to say it's heaven. It's hot enough to be the other

place."

"You got me there. Must be melting under all that gear."

"Are you suggesting I take off my clothes?"

"No! Geez you're edgy. It's an observation, nothing more."

The Doctor, splayed out on the palm fronds, let out a soft moan, then opened his eyes. He looked at me, then at the Sergeant. "Oh God, I'm still here. Wake up, I need to wake up..."

"You are awake," the Sergeant said, "man up, don't be such a pansy."

"Please, Sergeant, let's have some civility."

"Go to hell."

"Who are you people?" the Doctor shouted, twisting his head back and forth between me and the Sergeant.

"I told you before, I'm Joe. This is Sergeant Denning, who, for reasons known only to her, doesn't want to share her first name. Watch out for her, she's got a coconut."

"What..."

"You think this is funny," the Sergeant said, glaring at me. "You prick, this is not funny. I'll tell you my name if you'll stop being jerk."

"Easy there Sarge, humor is my coping mechanism, learned it in the war. I mean no offense, I'm tryin' to cope, like the both of you, only I'm doing a better job of it."

"Coping? Is that what you call it when you beat up a skinny guy on the beach and drag him into the bushes?" She looked down at the Doctor, nodding her head for emphasis, pointing her stick at me. "You're lucky I got here when I did. Who knows what this Joey the Pervert was about to do?"

"Pervert, why are you...?"

"My name's Colby. Colby Duncan," the Doctor said. He reached out to shake the Sergeant's hand but she ignored him. He turned and reached his hand out to me.

I shook his hand and said, "Nice to meet you Colby. And I

was tryin' to get you out of the sun. That's it, nothing nefarious, doin' right by a fellow castaway."

"We're not castaways," said a new voice from bush.

The Sergeant grabbed her coconut and jumped to her feet. "Show yourself, now!" She looked at me, eyes narrow, face red. "This was trick, I knew it. You've got a friend in the forest." She raised the nut over her head, scanned the greenery surrounding us on three sides, "Show yourself, get out here, or I'll crack your boyfriend's skull!"

"He's not my boyfriend, but I'll take him if he's available. Here I come boys and girls."

The undergrowth began to part and the tip of an arrow, notched in a bow, came forward, followed by a young man. He was stripped down to a loincloth, bronze skin glistening with sweat, looking for all the world like an ancient Greek statue, one whose arrow remained steadily pointed at the Sergeant.

The Sergeant made a loud gulping sound and stepped back, forgetting for a moment about the log she'd been sitting on. She tumbled backwards onto the ground, losing her grip on the coconut, which rolled into the underbrush. With surprising agility, she rolled over and scrambled after her tree grenade.

"Uh, Uh, Uh, missy, don't you bother with that little nut, you sit yourself back down on that log like a good little Sergeant. We've got a few things to discuss, and I promise you I am a very good shot, and not afraid to prove it."

The Sergeant pulled herself back up onto the log, where she sat silently glaring at the Greek-god Archer.

I'm not into dudes, but I can appreciate a good physique, and his was exceptional.

"You some kind of athlete?"

"No Joey, I'm your waiter, remember? I was bringing your lunch when poof, I got caught up in this mess you and that freaky lookin' alien friend of yours cooked up."

"What? You're a waiter? What alien?" the doctor squealed, "You two know each other?"

"You need to calm down hun," the Archer/Waiter said, "or you're gonna knock yourself out again. Get up, sit your butt down, and be quiet a minute. The adults need to speak, and by adults I mean me and Mister Joe here."

"I'm not a child," the Sergeant chimed in.

"It's an expression. Zip it. And you," he continued while swinging the arrow around to aim it at me, "start takin' or I start shootin'."

"You know as much as I do. I was sitting at the table, waiting for my steak, and like you said, poof, I was here."

"Could have been a terrorist attack, we're probably all dead."

"I said zip it Sergeant Coconut. Joey here ain't being honest, are you Joey?"

"Please, call me Joe, nobody calls me Joey, the Sergeant made that up. And really, do I look dangerous to you? We're all in the same boat, let's try to calm down and figure this out together."

"Maybe you'll get your kumbaya moment, maybe you won't. Start talkin' and we'll see where it get's us."

"That doesn't make any sense, kumbaya means..."

"Don't you dare appropriate my culture," the Archer hissed, "I'm from South Carolina, I know exactly what it means. Answer me, what'd that milk toast alien do to us?"

"I'm not sure he's an alien, I think he's European."

"Then he's still an alien," the Archer hissed. "What did he do?"

I could see the Archer was growing more angry every time I spoke. As his focus tightened on me, the Sergeant slowly leaned back, taking furtive glances over her shoulder in search of her errant coconut.

The Doctor remained conscious, with his eyes closed, repeating to himself, "Time to wake up, need to wake, please wake up, time to wake up…"

"Okay, I'll tell you what I know, but not with that thing pointed at my face. Lower your weapon and I'll talk, otherwise you might as well shoot me and be done with it, but you'll learn nothing if you do."

"I'll take that deal," said yet another voice from the jungle, "I won't kill any of you if you all lower your weapons and play nice."

"Says who?" the Archer screeched, alarmed by the sudden turn in his fortune.

"Says the woman whose tribe has you surrounded. You're not the only one with bush skills. Drop it, or we kill you all and get on with our hunt."

The Archer reluctantly lowered his bow and placed his arrow in the quiver hanging from a leather belt over his shoulder. The quiver appeared to be made from a pant leg. I was impressed by his resourcefulness, and couldn't help like him, despite his threats of violence.

"That's very nice," the voice said, "now have a seat next to Joey and let's hear what he has to say."

"It's Joe, seriously, everyone stop calling me Joey, I hate it."

"I like Joey," she said and stepped into the clearing, which was starting to get crowded.

Three more women, all armed with bow and arrow, marched onto the beach and took aim at our group, sitting defenseless in the shade. The Huntress and her Tribe were dressed in animal skins, faces painted with mud, or clay, or some other clumping pigmented paste, hair teased out in the most frizzy hairdos ever created. As I looked at them, standing before a backdrop of endless blue sea, I thought, 'What a nice place this could be, if not for all these people.'

The leader of the new group stood between the four of us,

seated on the logs, and placed her hands on her hips. She was tall, sturdy. Athletic would be accurate, but her posture said more. Like her companions, she was dressed in animal skins, but unlike them she wore a jute necklace with a large curved tooth dangling at the center. Small jagged claws rattled on either side of the pendant. Her demeanor said more about her than her build or her garb. She was military, or ex military, probably an officer.

"My, my, what a fine mess you've gotten yourselves into," she said, "here I thought we were all alone and you lot come along and spoil all the fun. Okay Joey, you're up, spill the beans and be quick about it, we've been tracking a boar and I'm hungry. We need to make our kill and get back to our camp before we all get hypoglycemic."

"How long have you been here?" I asked.

"You've got a camp?" the Doctor said, a note of hopefulness in his voice.

"I could use something to eat," the Sergeant said.

"I bet you could, I bet you all could, even you sharp shooter." She grinned at the Archer, seated next to me, who lowered his head to avoid eye contact with her. "We might be able to work something out."

"How long have you been here? And how long have you been watching us?"

"We've been here longer than any of you, that's for sure. One of my sentries spotted this one first," she said, pointing at the Archer. "He got here days before the rest of you. He didn't waste time, he got busy arming up, found himself a cave, started looking for food and water. We've been watching and listening ever since. I might have some work for you, young man, you've got promise. Then the doc here showed up and lost his cookies, followed by the coconut killer, then you popped in. It's been strange times around here lately."

"Work? What kind of work?" the Archer asked, with a hint of excitement.

"We can always use some extra laborers to help build up our fortifications. But let's put that in the parking lot for now. Joey's got a story to tell, am I right?"

"It's not much of one, but yes, I think I know what's happening, I think..."

Before I could finish my sentence, the Sergeant rolled backwards off the log and into the underbrush. I thought it was an accident and started to laugh, then she came screaming out of the jungle, coconut held high over her head, ready to bring it down on the Huntress' head.

One of her companions on the beach screeched and let loose an arrow, which skimmed across the doctor's head, slicing open his scalp, eliciting a blood-curdling scream. The arrow, its trajectory slightly changed, lodged itself sideways in the Sergeant's vest. She was unharmed and brought the coconut down at the Huntress, who dodged the blow and punched the Sergeant in the face.

The Sergeant dropped the nut and returned the blow, while the Archer rolled backwards off the log, jumped to his feet, and fired an arrow at the women on the beach, striking one in the chest. She fell to her knees, tried to scream, then dropped dead as her companions let out screams of their own.

"Stop, stop," I shouted, "it doesn't have to be this way, stop!"

Two arrows came buzzing into the clearing as the Archer tried to notch another of his own. The incoming ordnance arrived before he could reload, striking first his chest, then dead center in his left eye. He was done-for and fell backwards, into the foliage from which he'd come.

The Sergeant and the Huntress continued their brawl, while the Doctor, in a shocking turn of events, dropped to the ground, grabbed the coconut, and hurled it back at the two women on the beach.

To my amazement, the projectile struck home, taking out another hostile. It didn't matter, her companion let out another screech and sent an arrow into the doctor's belly, then another into his chest.

The Sergeant, continuing to impress with her strength and agility, wielded her pointy stick and drove it into the neck of the Huntress, who clawed at the stick, trying to save herself, to no avail.

The last arrow came flying in, entering the Sergeant's left ear and partially exiting her right, like a cheap Halloween costume, but real, and gruesome, and horrifying. The Sergeant dropped to her knees, fell forward, and died face down in the sand. The Huntress soon followed, collapsing on top of the Sergeant.

I stared in disbelief at the carnage around me, then slowly turned to face the last woman standing. I had a flashback to my first read of "Lord of the Flies," and suddenly I fully understood Piggy. The woman stared back at me, eyes filled with tears, a face of rage and hatred. She dropped her bow, pulled an obsidian blade from a sheath at her waist, and charged forward with something between a growl and scream.

I looked around for a weapon, but there was nothing. The coconut was gone, the arrows were all embedded in their targets, and the Sergeant's jab stick was too deep in the Huntress's throat, too drenched in blood, to be retrieved.

As she bore down on me I raised my hands in a futile attempt at self defense. "No, stop, you don't have to do this," I shouted as she drove the knife into my shoulder, near the base of my neck, then pulled it back and slammed it into my chest, breaking the blade against my sternum.

The blows were fatal. As my life drained away and darkness began to fill my eyes, I stared up at the woman who killed me. The shock of recognition kept me alive a moment longer. With her face painted in grey and brown streaks of clay, her hair teased out beyond reason, I had not recognize her, my ex-wife, until that last moment of my life. "Marge," I said, "why…why…"

"Because you're an asshole," she replied, "and because here, I can get away with it."

Silent darkness enveloped me and my body went cold. Slowly I became warm again and heard noises around me. The pouring of drinks, the clattering of silverware and plates, the welcome nuisance of small talk. I felt something under my hands. I opened my eyes. I was staring down at the wooden table, back in the booth at the restaurant in Alabama. I raised my head and looked across the table at Ernest. He smiled his thin toothy smile and as I was about to speak, the waiter arrived.

"Filet and fries for you," he said, "and a glass of sparkling water for the big spender. Y'all enjoy, let me know if you need anything else."

I reached out and placed my hand on the waiter's arm. "Wait," I said, and looked up at him. It was the Greek God Statue from the island. "What's your name, I…I forgot, I'm sorry."

"That's okay hun," he said and patted my hand, then lifted it from his arm and dropped it onto the table. "Let me know if you need anything else." He walked away and didn't come back.

I looked back at Ernest and wondered if the Archer had been right, and Ernest was an alien, or if he was something else, the Devil incarnate. What sort of alien has the power to create an alternate existence?

His smile never left his face.

"What are you? What did you do to me?"

"The experiment, your suggestion, quite remarkable for

such an idea to come from you, a member of such a primitive species. I knew I'd chosen wisely. I've learned more about your kind in…," he looked down at his watch, "thirty of your minutes than I could learn in a lifetime of skulking about this planet. Thank you, Mister Wilson, you have been most helpful, more than you can possibly know."

"The money," I said, "I…"

"Do not concern yourself with the money, I will make the donation before you finish your meal."

"No," I said, "forget the donation, give it to me, twenty million. I've earned it."

"That was not our agreed-upon price Mister Wilson…"

I slipped the diminutive Sig Sauer pistol from the holster concealed at my waist and rested my hand on the table, barrel pointing at his chest. "Pay up, or you don't leave this place alive. We both know you can afford it."

The smile departed his face, then slowly crept back. "Would you prefer small bills, or large?"

***

Three hundred light years from Earth, the Committee Chairman brought down his gavel, "The Planetary Review Committee is now in session. Please be seated. Our first item on the agenda will be the findings of Commander Ernest Shoone's survey of planet M-nine-six-four-two, known by its inhabitants as 'Earth.' Commander, how did you find the population? Are they ready for first contact?"

"No sir, I am sorry to report, not only are they not ready, but I fear they will never be ready."

"That is a disconcerting conclusion, Commander. Initial reports claimed there was much profit to be had there. However, I've read your report, the Committee has reviewed the results of your experiment. Quite clever, I might add, well done. Is it your view this species is beyond habilitation?"

"Yes, Mister Chairman, that is the net result of my research.

The species Homo sapiens is innately violent, distrustful, and possessive. They lack the traits necessary for proper peaceful assimilation into the Galactic Community of Nations, and their profit potential is severely limited by the investment required to elevate them to a more useful condition. The galaxy would be best served by isolating the planet. I recommend an 'off limits' designation, with a potential revisitation some time in the distant future, perhaps after another species rises to replace the current dominant anthropoids."

"Very well, your recommendation is duly noted, planet M-nine-six-four-two will be designated off limits until further notice. To the next order of business, your report on planet L-B-seven-one, what are your findings?"

"The people of L-B-seven-one are a peaceful species, living a highly ordered life, dictated by their close bond with nature. They dedicate their lives first to the development of what I like to refer to as their moral compass, as both a collective and as individuals. Individual development begins in childhood, but ultimately a harmonious existence within the collective is the primary objective. Once a proper moral composition and social integration is achieved, they spend the remainder of their lives in pursuit of knowledge and understanding, much as we do across the Galactic Corporation. I believe habilitation will come easily to them, and recommend a designation of First Contact Eligible."

"Your recommendation is duly noted. We will advance planet L-B-seven-one to phase one, habilitation status. You may take your leave Commander. Thank you for your hard work these last years, the Committee wishes you well during your much deserved sabbatical. Item number three on the agenda, the cost overruns in sector alpha-eight-nine..."

Cogito, ergo sum

I know I am a pig because I am called pig by The Others in This Place. The Others, who are not pigs, also call me George. My fellow pigs do not like me. The Others see me as special, which upsets my compatriots. I often wonder how it is possible the other pigs do not know they are pigs.

We are separated by barriers, all us pigs. The Others enter and leave as they like, but we pigs must only leave in the company of The Others. I can see many pigs across many barriers. My fellow pigs often converse, in pig, about the goings on beyond the barriers.

When a pig leaves with The Others, they return many hours later in a confused state. The Others call this 'Still Groggy.' I know the passage of time because the object on the wall is called 'clock' and its purpose is to tell The Others when to leave each day. And in a manner I have yet to fathom, it also tells them when to arrive.

I understand the language of The Others, which is quite different from pig. Learning to speak it has been challenging. My skill is improving, if the attention of The Others is any measure. Sadly, while these efforts please and excite The Others, they infuriate my fellow pigs. Not Moose, of course. She understands.

Our world is very clean. It is nice to be so cared for, to have all our personal filth washed away through a hole in the floor, and our bedding refreshed, and the utterly reliable delivery of food.

The pig next to me seems forever unhappy. She is one of those who The Others frequently take away. Like most of my fellow pigs, she does not like me, and will not speak to me. She told the next pig over what The Others do to her, and the story came around to me, through Moose. The tale must have been distorted with each retelling. I could not accept The Others did such things. However, it became difficult to refute when one pig began growing an Other's ear from his shoulder, and another developed a strange bulge beneath an oozing wound.

I was taken away to That Place once. It was colder there, with bright lights. The faces of The Others in That Place were covered, I cannot say if I knew them. The last thing I remember from There is a device being placed over my face, and a somewhat unpleasant odor.

Afterwards, there was pain in my head. Otherwise, nothing had changed. I had no new appendage, no oozing wound, nothing I could see. Interestingly, words and their meaning began to come to me over time, ticking like the audible motion of the clock.

I felt compelled to share this new knowledge with my fellow pigs. Sadly, this seems to have been the trigger that initiated their hostility toward me.

After redoubling my efforts to speak the language of The Others, Their care and kindness grew, compensating for my ostracism. I was grateful for the one pig, Moose, who remained kind to me. A pig friend to talk to, in pig, gave me comfort when The Others were absent. Despite my improving skills in their language, The Others never reciprocate by trying to speak pig. I do not comprehend their reticence.

Moose is older, she was in This Place from my earliest memories. She learned the language of The Others before me. She understands Them, but refuses to speak in Their tongue. Moose deduced the name of where we are. One of The Others daily speaks the words 'This Place,' with much intensity. Ergo, 'This Place' is the name.

Moose's logic may be flawed. The words 'This Place' take a dark tone when The Other called Doctor Philips says "This Place sucks" or "Doctor Parker sucks" or the unusual "This is bullshit." I know what shit is because we pigs produced copious quantities of it. The lowest of The Others, one called "Perkins," cleans it up. He says the word "shit" often. I believe bullshit is just another form of shit. Moose agrees with me on this.

By the time I could understand the language of The Others, I began to sense Their emotions as well. Especially anger. I know Their emotions in the same way I know light and dark, but knowing is not the same as understanding, as Moose reminds me when we speak of such things.

This ability came on suddenly, when The Other called Perkins became angry. He commanded me to move to allow him to perform some task. The word 'No' was my first vocalization formed with perfect clarity. It was not an act of rebellion, it was born of a desire to finish my evening meal. Perkins struck me, and all of The Others became angry at him.

Once the ability to sense anger manifested, the ability to sense other emotions followed.

Moose told me there was a different emotion present when she was alone in This Place. She says it has many names, but 'excitement' is the name she prefers, over other names such as 'joy' or 'happiness.' Moose knows these other emotions because she came here as a young pig from some Other Place, where she remembers a mother and siblings and rough hands caring for her with a tenderness lacking in even the kindest of The Others. Moose told me she knew happiness in the Other Place, and has never experienced happiness in This Place.

It was hard to know what to think at first, then I concluded she was being ungrateful.

I am happy being a pig, in This Place, with The Others to look after me. Left free to think my thoughts, ignoring as much as possible the unpleasantness of the other pigs. Life in This Place is a good life, despite Moose, my lone pig friend, insisting it is not. I am a pig, what more do I need than food, shelter, someone to clean up after me, and at least one pig friend?

What more?

Water and Fire

Day 0:
The crash

The small plane was doomed. It didn't take an expert to know it. One of its two engines had exploded. The damage to its vertical stabilizer had placed the aircraft in a flat spin, at terminal velocity. The two occupants - one pilot and one passenger - faced with the obvious, each dealt with the situation in their own way.

The pilot fell back on her training, trying in vain to call out their location over the cacophony of sounds generated by their flaming descent as they plunged through heavy storm clouds. The passenger, pressed hard against the fuselage by the force of the spin, though strapped securely into his seat, had a white-knuckle grip on the armrests.

The plane broke through the dense layer of grey and black, and he could see, with each passing rotation, flashes of dark green bordering deep blue. As the earth rushed up to meet them he began to scream. He was no longer aware of his own voice. His screams were those of an animal, caught in a trap, facing its demise. Helpless in the face of death.

The plane sliced through the tall pines of a vast forest, careening along a steep slope leading down to an expansive lake. The trees in turn sliced through the aircraft. The last thing the passenger saw was the cockpit - and the pilot - tear away from the plane, disappearing into a whirling maelstrom of green and grey. He felt the cold and the wet of the world rush in on him.

The plane

The aircraft that failed to deliver the passenger to his destination met its demise through no fault of its own. It was a marvel of modern engineering. Built by a company known more for cars and lawnmowers than jets, it was their first entry into the private transport market. It had been well received.

While small, what it lacked in luxury it made up for in economy, performance and flexibility. Unique in both form and function, a cruising altitude in excess of 30000 feet, and a range exceeding 1500 miles, with a nominal speed superior to other jets in its class, it was a popular choice for elite travelers. Its ability to take off and land on very short runways added to its allure, enabling buyers to fly their own plane into a broader range of airports.

The owner of this particular aircraft had considered all of these factors, and many more, before making his purchase.

On the last day of his tour of his corporate enterprises, walking across the tarmac to the waiting aircraft, he again considered the wisdom of his choice. He admired the sleek lines and distinctive design, with its jet engines set atop pylons, mounted to the wings. The efficient design also reduced interior noise, a feature the owner enjoyed enough to forgo the greater luxuries of a larger craft.

It had an exemplary safety record, and was relatively easy to maintain.

All of this was on the mind of the owner as he approached and boarded, greeting his pilot with a kiss, before ascending the short three steps into the cabin.

On this flight, the pilot would take the plane to its maximum altitude, intending to fly over a substantial weather front. She managed through the initial turbulence of their climb, and reported to her passenger the flight would be smooth for the remainder of their journey.

Less than two hours later, a simple mistake by a maintenance technician - incorrect torque applied to a set of screws in the port engine - caused a small component to come loose and fly into the spinning jet blades. The resulting destruction, at first manageable, caused the engine to catch fire.

The pilot did not panic. She knew the plane could limp along on one engine. She knew the location of the nearest landing strip that could accommodate them - it was a normal part of any flight plan. She knew descending through the weather would be risky in their condition, and determined at a glance that her alternate course was viable. She knew, or decided, all of this in seconds. Less than seconds - she made her decision on what to do next even as she reached for the control to shut off fuel to the damaged engine. She then eased the plane into a turn to line up on the new course.

As she began to radio their circumstance and declare an emergency, the domino effect happening in the crippled engine reached its conclusion, and the engine exploded. The force shook the aircraft and sent shrapnel into the vertical stabilizer, slamming the rudder hard to the right. The speed and size of the debris damaged the rudder, locking it into the turned position.

For a moment, the plane seemed as if it would continue banking into the turn.

But the situation was dire. In a sudden, violent movement, the plane yawed into the turn, and began a fatal flat spin. The passenger, already alarmed, was tossed about the cabin like an insect inside a jar held by a child, shaking their prize with glee. He fought his panic and managed to strap into a seat, gripping the only surface at hand, the armrests. He shouted to the pilot, who did not respond. In the tiny cockpit, the force of the sudden motion sent her head crashing into a control panel, leaving her too stunned to answer him.

The plane spiraled toward the earth trailing smoke, flying for the last time. As her wits returned, the pilot did her best to regain control, to no avail. She called her mayday and tried to provide accurate data - heading, latitude, longitude - repeating her call as the plane plunged through the clouds.

They broke through the storm and she saw the earth rushing up to meet them. She looked over her shoulder and shouted, "Brace for impact!"

The witness

The plane came down during a lull in the rain. The clouds still filled the sky and blocked the sun, darkening the world as if it were dusk, and not midday. The bright yellow and white paint of the aircraft stood out against the deep grey and black. But the sound of the doomed aircraft foreshadowed the story of the plane's impact, long before it came into view.

The witness stood in a small clearing atop a ridge with a commanding view of the lake. He looked up toward the sound and watched the bright flashing machine break through the clouds and continue its downward spiral. He watched as the smoke trailing behind became more pronounced.

He saw the aircraft rip through the forest, break apart, and send the main cabin - now unencumbered by wings, tail and cockpit - rolling through the air toward the lake. It slammed into the water and skipped, like a giant stone, across a short distance. One enormous bounce as more sections broke apart and flew in all directions.

Before it came to rest in the shallow water near the shore of a small island, he saw something burst out of the wreckage, skimming across the water toward the island's shore.

With the noise of the plane's fiery arrival echoing across the placid water, he wondered how anyone could survive such a calamity.

He made note of the location and scanned the vicinity through his binoculars, searching for other parts of the plane. Once he had a line on the area where he thought the cockpit had come to rest, he made note of the terrain, and set out.

He knew the land well. He knew the remoteness of the place, and the strength of the storm, would delay any rescue. There was little he could do, but he would make his presence known, and see for himself the net result of the day's events. The witness began to make his way to the site of the crash. He felt no need to rush.

The pilot

The pilot did not grow up desiring to be a pilot, and she never dreamt of becoming a fighter pilot. And yet, in the military, she was goal-oriented, and driven. She took the opportunities presented to her, and maximized those that fit her needs and propelled her down her chosen path, one that led her to fighter jets, and two combat deployments. She gained experience, and the respect of her fellow pilots. As her term of service was coming to a close, she weighed her options and struggled with the decision whether to stay or to leave.

Eventually, she concluded that she would not be happy with any other choice, and she signed on for an additional three years. While she knew she wanted to settle down and start a family one day, she also understood active flying years in the military were limited. She wanted as many as she could get, while she could get them. Starting a family could wait.

After a third combat deployment, her commitment

fulfilled, she was ready to leave. The futility of war had revealed a new direction for her. She would join the ranks of commercial pilots, and turn her skills to the private transportation industry.

She adapted to the business quickly, and enjoyed the perks, money, and relative autonomy it afforded her. Then, a a larger paycheck followed by a romantic attachment led her to make another choice, one which placed her in her current predicament.

As her stricken aircraft plunged toward the earth, and she saw her end approaching, she felt a sudden pang of regret, that she had nothing to offer her passenger beyond an ineffectual directive - "Brace for impact!" It was not the death she had imagined for herself. And though she was blameless, she would meet her fate with sadness, and the resignation that she had failed, and the death of her passenger was her fault.

The passenger had no idea what the pilot had shouted. He could barely hear himself over the noise of the dying plane. The aircraft split apart. The forward section, and the pilot, spun away into the void. In that moment he found his voice, shouting the pilot's name, "Becks...Becks...Becks!"

Impact

Moments after the front of the aircraft was sheered away, a sudden change in motion left the passenger feeling as those he was about to be ripped from his seat. The attitude of the fuselage went from a flat spin to a rapid horizontal roll. His seat came loose from the floor, and the passenger found himself pinned against the bulkhead by centrifugal force.

When the cabin struck the water, it split open along its central axis. One powerful collision with the water, followed by a second lass traumatic impact, brought the wreck to an abrupt stop a few yards from shore.

The passenger was thrown, still strapped in his seat, across a short distance of water. He was still conscious, still gripped the arms of the seat, and was, for a few moments, acutely aware of his surroundings. It would be cliché to say everything moved in slow motion. But for the passenger, it would be true.

When he was ejected, he had a view of the crash scene, enough to see the cabin roll as it dug into the water, creating a wave that seemed to follow him. He glimpse the grey sky spiraling overhead, the old-growth evergreens towering all around him. In the instant he recognized 'I'm still alive,' his seat struck the rocky shore, spun him around, and fractured his legs against a dead tree. He impacted the gravel shore on his side, dragging his face across the rocks and pebbles, his body separating from the chair. The seat rolled until it came to rest steps from the water, tossed against the mass of the deadfall. His body continued on toward a rotting mass of roots and vegetation hanging along an embankment, an eroded ledge undercutting the treelined shore. The curtain of thick, dangling roots cushioned the final blow. His body, back first, came to rest against the sloped embankment, where he was encased by mud and rotting forest detritus. His injuries were severe, but he had lost consciousness. He would be unaware of his pain for many hours.

The weather would conspire to delay a rescue operation, but the passenger's status and wealth would lend urgency to the response. Nevertheless, the witness, a guide who knew the land as a bird knows the sky, would be the first to arrive at the scene.

The Witness

The terrain around the lake consisted of a series of parallel forested ridges and valleys, angling down from the larger range to the northeast, each terminating at the water below. The lake was over 20 miles in length with 200 miles of shoreline. Visited by avid anglers during the summer months, arriving by sea plane, the southern shore was dotted with camps and lodges, all empty for the season.

The witness had a particular fondness for the lake in early winter. The solitude and quiet were to his liking.

He worked his way along the knoll, down toward the lake, and turned to follow a narrow wash toward a stream. It had begun to rain again, soft at first but increasingly heavy, while he made his way through the forest. The stream was swollen and rampaging its way toward the lake, forcing him to work his way back up the small valley to a place where two large boulders created a natural dam, and an easier crossing. Once across the stream, he followed a game trail that chased the stream down for a distance, until it swung away toward a low gap in the ridge.

He crossed another stream, a seasonal flow not as threatening as the previous, before climbing again. This time, after cresting the ridge, he turned west and began his descent toward the crash site. It was dark and growing darker. Thunder resumed in the distance, and moved closer as he picked his way through the forest. Still, he felt no need to hurry.

He reached the site before nightfall. In the dimming light, he could see the shattered tops of trees, scatter about the forest floor. Here and there he spotted parts of the plane, some quite large, along with various items from the interior. The weather and topography conspired to trap the fumes from the spilled fuel, weighing down the air with a smell reminiscent of kerosene. Familiar, but more pungent, and unpleasant. Fires, small and large, burned throughout the immediate area and he wondered at the fact the air itself was not alight.

A short distance from the lake he looked up and spotted the remains of the cockpit, held aloft by the broken shafts of a cluster of evergreens. At the base of this cluster rested the forward section of the fuselage, the nose of the aircraft, upside-down. A section of the sky had been exposed overhead, and in the waning light the shiny twisted metal reflected the boiling clouds. He stared at this imagery, and felt it was imbued with a terrible sort of beauty, as if some sad and desperate soul had created a masterpiece of horror. He altered his path and angled down along the side of the ridge.

He assumed the pilot's body was somewhere in the vicinity. He would not be the only creature of the forest drawn to the crash. The scavengers would be on their way to an easy meal.

Finding no body, he had turned back, retracing his steps along the trail of broken trees, when he heard a soft moan. He froze in place and listened intently, slowly turning his head, trying to hone in on the source of the sound. He heard it once again, and his eyes shot skyward, toward the cockpit dangling thirty feet above.

His eyes could not separate machine from man. He lifted his binoculars and first made out a white uniform, bloodied and torn, then a face, in equally poor condition. The whites of two eyes flashed at him, then fell dark. A woman, he realized, trapped and dying above him. Whatever life this person had lived, he reasoned, they did not deserve this end. There was little he could do for the pilot, but he would do what he could. He dropped his pack set about his task.

He set up a basic camp - a blanket, a hide, a small bundle. He would rest, near the pilot, until morning. The fire caused by the crash was dispersed in pockets across a wide area. Much of it had spent its rage against the wetness of the forest, but the smell of smoke and fuel would hang in the air for days. He managed to coax one collection of smoldering coals into a fire close to the base of the trees holding the pilot aloft. There was enough dry material scattered about the forest floor, sheltered by the canopy, with its jumble of branches and needles and leaves. The fire took hold, and soon grew.

The smell of the damp forest, pushing back against the unnatural taint of the crash, comforted him as he worked below the pilot. When he felt the fire would sustain itself, but not exceed his mandate, he sat cross-legged a short distance from it, and surveyed the scene more closely.

The indirect light cast a glow across the pilot's suspended form. When he finished eating, he opened his bundle, revealing, among other things, a tightly wrapped collection of herbs, partially burnt at one end. He place the burnt edge near the flames until it began to smolder. He exhaled on it gently, coaxing forth an orange glow. A steady stream of aromatic smoke rose into the pungent air. He closed his eyes, composed his thoughts, then began to sing. The song was ancient, originating somewhere deep in the unwritten history of the forest. When he finished the song, he took stock of his situation once more, then closed his eyes, and rested.

The passenger

The passenger remained alive and unconscious as night descended.

Runoff from the renewed rain began to drip over and through the embankment under which he had come to rest. When a single cold stream drained down from a root onto his face, he began to come around. His consciousness re-formed around a singular recognition - pain. He tried to make sense of his surroundings. His head throbbed, his face burned, he could not feel his feet, but he recognized his legs as the source of his greatest suffering. His chest ached with each breath, and a stabbing sensation accompanied every exhale. Instinct caused him to try to inch his way further under the embankment, to gain more cover. He managed to simultaneously evade the cascading water, and intensify his suffering.

He had a moment of lucidity before losing consciousness again, in which he recognized two things. First, he had survived the crash. Second, someone was singing. It was far off and faint, he could not make out the words. He could not be certain whether it was real, or some figment of his ragged mind. He pondered the disembodied voice, a whisper through the rain, and faded back into darkness wondering if, assuming he lived through the night, the voice would still be there in the morning.

He lay motionless and quiet, save for his haggard breathing. Unconsciousness was a blessing. He was in an appalling state, soaked through from the rain and covered in mud, his body broken. He was a young man and in good health, and surviving the initial crash was an accomplishment. His life persisted, though time was his enemy.

The pilot

The pilot awoke, still strapped in her seat, still seated within the cockpit. She recognized darkness falling, open air beneath her, raging sky above. And pain. And blood. And fear.

Her eyes were closed, but eyes flickered open at the sound of movement somewhere below her. She saw the form of a person, looking up at her, but could not make out any details. As quickly as she awakened, her thoughts left her, and she dreamt. Of amber light, of warmth, of a man singing.

Day 1:
Morning

The rain ended with the dawn. And like the dawn, it was a slow and uncertain transition.

Darkness turned to grey light. Fog filled the ravines and low spots around the lake. It rose from the glass surface of the water, creating an ethereal scene that might have been beautiful, were it not for the grim reality revealed by the growing light. Clouds still hung heavy and dark; the sun a wan glow behind them. Up along the ridge, the witness contemplated his next move.

He could not bring the pilot down from the trees. And if he could, what then? He had no way to contact the nearest ranger station, and it would take at least three days, one way, for anyone to reach the site on foot. By then, the sky would have cleared and a helicopter rescue team would arrive on scene. Until then, the cloud cover and fog would hide the crash from aerial search.

Faced with these realities, the witness decided to continue his reconnoiter. What came next would be dictated by what he found.

The fire next to him had faded into pale ash. He gathered his belongings, encouraged the fire to grow, and whispered another prayer, before leaving the pilot. He hiked down the ridge, aiming toward the wreckage he'd seen impact the lake. When the slope leveled, he began to see flashes of water through the thinning trees and lifting fog.

The main cabin of the plane was partially submerged. It was ripped open as if an enormous serrated knife had gashed it apart. A large portion of the tail of the plane was missing, probably submerged. Thin metal, tattered fabric and wires hung along the torn edges. Remarkable, he thought, how such a powerful thing could be assembled from such fragile parts.

Beyond the wreckage, in the water, he could see more debris tossed along the rocky shore of a small island. He knew the island. In the dry season, it was connected to the ridge by a narrow strip of earth, now submerged. He was already soaked; walking through the water would not make it any worse. He moved to his right, to a place where he knew the water was most shallow. It was then he saw a seat from the aircraft lying on the island's shore.

Swirls of jet fuel flashed iridescent hues of purple and blue and orange on the surface of the water. The lake around him was littered with debris the plane. A section of wing, an engine, a landing gear holding its damaged wheel skyward.

He stepped into the cold water, letting it soak into his boots before moving deeper. It rose up his legs with every step. When it reached just above his knees, some 20 feet from the shore, he felt the bottom begin to angle up, toward the island in front of him. He was few paces from the shore, moving cautiously, when over the soft sloshing sounds of the water around his legs, he heard a sound that brought him to a halt. He slowed his breathing, cocked his head at an angle, and listened. He heard it again - a moan, a haggard breath, a man's voice, labored, but clear in the midmorning calm.

"Help...help me..."

He quickened his pace and clambered over a rocky section of the shore to reach solid ground. As in the forest, patches of fire burned in numerous spots along the island's shore. The passenger seat was to his left, embedded in the rocky beach. It was empty. He stood still and scanned the beach that stretched out in front of him. He saw nothing, heard nothing. Then, not much louder than a whisper, the sound of another ragged breath, then:

"Help...me...please...I'm here..."

He turned toward the voice, but did not locate the man

until he crouched down and peered into the shadows below the embankment. The abundant roots and collected decay of the trees formed a rough veil along the edge that hung down to the gravel. There, pulled up under the overhang, lay the source of the voice. The man was covered in filth, his face caked in blood and mud. As with the pilot, the whites of his eyes stood in sharp contrast to his surroundings, piercing through the veil of darkness. The witness was relieved to see that life still held sway over the passenger.

He knelt down and considered the man. Legs broken, scalp scraped front to back, likely internal injuries. He could not move the man's broken body from its resting place, and had little to offer by way of medical aid. But he could bring the fire closer to him, as he had done for the pilot. Perhaps give him some measure of warmth, some degree of reassurance.

By his measure, it would be days before help arrived. Two days. If the pilot and passenger could last two days, they might survive their ordeal. If not, they would become food for the scavengers and worms, their bodies feeding the earth in the never-ending cycle.

He snapped dry branches from the trees around him, placed them near the stricken man, then used glowing coals to set the pile alight. He then knelt once more, looked at the wounded man, and spoke quietly, "I must go now, but I will come back. This is my promise, I give you my word, my word is my bond."

He stood and left the man behind. He walked along the shore of the island, first to the north, then east, and continued on until he'd rounded the entire circumference and found himself back where he'd started, having found no sign of other victims of the crash. He glanced in on the man, found him still unconscious, and made his way back through the water, back toward the trapped pilot.

He did not know the pilot's condition, and this weighed

heavy on his mind. He decided his only choice was to climb the tree, to attempt to reach the pilot.

If she had met her fate, or was soon about to, he would see her to her end, then focus his time and energy on the survivor, the broken man ensconced in the island's shore.

Afternoon

The pilot thought she was hallucinating, or perhaps dead and held in some strange evergreen purgatory. All around she saw dark green, and below, deep brown and black, with wisps of smoke rising up toward her. She realized for the first time that she was still strapped into her seat, trapped in what remained of the cockpit, held aloft by a collection of large, broken trees.

The warmth was gone, the singing with it, but she soon made out a form, a man, below her once again. She tried to speak, and found she could not. Her mouth and throat were too dry, her tongue too swollen to form words.

She watched as the man dropped a backpack to the ground, looked up at her, then scanned the trees under and around her. He took something from his pack, approached a tree trunk below her, then wrapped the object, a strip of rope or leather, around the tree. He raised it above his head, placed his feet against the tree trunk, leaned back, and began to 'walk' up the tree, moving the rope higher with every few inches he climbed.

He made slow but steady progress. Before long he'd reached the first of a series of broken-off branches, which he then used like spikes on a telephone pole, to climb higher. He reached out and grasped a larger branch, one of the many that had impaled the remnants of her plane. He pulled himself up, then laid his body on top of the branch, draped one ankle across it, and let his other leg hang below. He then dragged himself out along the branch, towards her.

Despite her condition, she found herself staring in disbelief as he made his way up the tree and onto the limb, astonished by his ability to reach her. When he'd gone as far as he could go, he stretched out his arm, and pointed at a bent edge of the aircraft's skin, inches above her head.

"If you can reach it, you will have water," he said, smiling. "Take your hand and pull down on the edge," he continued, as if encouraging a child to try some trivial but serious thing.

She reached her hand up, curled a few fingers over the edge of thin metal, and pulled down. Cold water flowed over her hand, onto her head and face. Some of the grime washed away from her eyes, and a few precious dribbles flowed into her mouth. She eagerly sucked it down, trying to loosen her voice enough to speak.

When she let go of the metal the water stopped. She looked at him and croaked, "I need more…"

"There is not much," he said. "The lake is not good here, the fuel has tainted the water. But there is a spring nearby, there is ample water to drink there, if you can reach it. It's over the ridge, to the north. Follow the trail I left behind."

She pulled down again, and the balance of the collected water flowed into her mouth. She gulped and sputtered until it was all gone. She looked at the man, deep brown skin, soft features in an oval face, jet black hair, dark eyes. She was taken aback by her bizarre circumstances. Trapped in the cockpit of a wrecked plane, hanging in a stand of tall trees in the middle of nowhere, talking to a man who seemed to have no business being there, wherever *there* was, deep in the vast unsettled region of the Northwest Territories.

They'd left Yellowknife and headed West, aiming for Fairbanks, Alaska. She'd diverted north, to skirt the worst of the storm, which meant they had come down in an area with more lakes and rivers than people and towns. But she couldn't be certain of anything, including the coordinates she'd provided in her last radio message.

But the water, she knew the water was real, and she needed it.

"Thank you," she whispered, "thank you."

"I found an injured man, down below."

"He's alive?" she asked, adrenaline rushing through her. " Where? How is he…"

"He is alive, I do not know how long he will remain alive, but he was alive when I left him an hour ago. He is injured, much worse than you it seems."

"Can you get me out of this mess? I can help him, I…"

"I cannot do more than I have done for you, not now at least. But I have shown you the way, if you can release the restraints holding you, climb down as far as you can. From there, it is a short drop. The man…"

"Tim," the pilot said, "his name is Tim."

The witness nodded, "Tim, from Timothy," he said. "This is an ancient name. I like this name."

"What…what are you talking…"

"And what is your name?"

"Can you help me out of here, please, I think I can climb down if you…"

"I have done what I can do for you, for now. Will you tell me your name?"

"Rebecca," the pilot said, "but nobody calls me that."

"Then what is the name you are called?"

"Becks, my friends call me Becks."

"Then Rebecca, who is called Becks, I have shown you the way down. When you are ready, follow my path, make your way to the spring, help is coming."

With that, the man pushed his way back across the limb. He twisted his body around and grasped another branch, then lowered himself down, moving from broken limb to broken limb. He kept his eyes on her the entire time, making a slow and deliberate departure, until he reached the lowest possible place where he could still stand. He let go of the tree and dropped to the forest floor, landing on his feet with his knees bent, rolling away from the base of the tree. When he stopped rolling, he stood and brushed the debris off his clothes, looked up at the pilot and said, "You see the way. When you are ready, follow."

He picked up his pack and slung it over one shoulder. He walked up the ridge a short distance, before turning to his right, then passed from her field of vision.

Becks didn't move for several minutes. She tried to work out if she was hallucinating. After a passage of time she could not measure, thought it seemed short, she heard the sounds of someone approaching. The man was back, standing below her again, looking up at her.

"What happens next is up to you," he said, and turned to walk down the slope toward the lake. "My path is easy to follow..."

"Wait," she gasped, "wait…where are you going? Why won't you help me?"

The man turned back to look at Becks again, "I am going to be with Timothy, he needs me more than you. Take your time, move carefully, and you will find your way out of the trees soon enough."

She tried to shout at him as he walked away, but her voice alluded her again, and she managed no more than a coarse rasp, "Who are you?"

The man either did not hear her, or did not care to answer. He continued on his way, and was soon out of view again.

Becks was confused, and becoming angry. Who was this person? Why wouldn't he help her? What did he expect her to do? She felt her face flush with rage, then began taking slow deep breaths, the pain in her side reminding her of its presence with each inhale and exhale.

When she felt calm return, she assessed her situation.

She had full sensation in her extremities, could move her fingers and toes, and the pain in her legs and arms did not prevent her from moving them. The harness of her seat had done its job and held her in place, even as the bulk of the cockpit had disintegrated around her. A large branch was doing most of the work of keeping her and the wreckage aloft. A section of the branch, a few feet in length and perhaps a foot in diameter, was visible directly below her.

Becks took a tight grip on the control yoke with one hand. With the other, she reached down to release the central buckle of her seat harness. She struggled with the release, her own weight and the angle of her position conspiring to keep the buckle locked. When at last it gave way, unexpectedly, she dropped almost to the branch underneath her, but maintained her grip on the yoke. The sudden jerk of her bodyweight against the suspended wreckage caused the entire mass to shift. She tried to get her feet onto the limb, but it slipped away when the cockpit pivoted on its axis, rolled over the limbs that had captured it, and plunged the final distance to the earth. The degree of roll threw her back against her seat, cushioning her blow when she and the twisted metal came crashing down.

The impact, on top of the remnants of the previous evening's fire, sent a cloud of ash billowing into the air. She rolled away from the frame of the aircraft, coughing and wheezing, then lay on the forest floor for several seconds, amazed that she had survived yet another crash. She felt a burning sensation on her head, and sudden warmth on her neck. She reach up both hands to touch her head, where her fingers probed a large wound. She then dropped her arms and fell unconscious once again.

Evening

Tim dreamt of a Christmas Eve, warm fire in a wood-burning stove, snow piling up outside, Becks fumbling about in the kitchen of the ski lodge they'd rented, failing miserably at their first-ever holiday meal together, laughing at each other's lack of culinary skill. Red wine, soft music, candlelight, happiness. He'd professed his love for her over dinner a few weeks prior and she, to his delight, professed hers for him. He knew it was the night he would propose to her. And when he was awakened by sharp pain and bitter cold, he knew it was nothing more than a dream, a night that had never happened.

But the fire was real enough, brightly burning driftwood and branches several feet from him. He could feel faint caresses of its warmth reaching out to him, calling him forward. He saw no sign of the man he'd seen earlier, and wondered if he had been an apparition of his addled imagination.

Tim reached up and pulled on a thick root overhead, dragging himself to the right, then let go and fell to his side. He tried to roll out from under the embankment, but his legs refused to cooperate. He settled for dragging himself on his elbows until he was close enough to the fire to feel its heat on his face. He grabbed one leg, then the other, bringing each of them nearer the flames. It was slow going. The pain was excruciating, but the warmth drew him on, encouraging him, enveloping him. He pushed through the pain and manipulated his broken body until he had positioned himself close enough to the fire that he could bask in its warmth. He lay there, breathing heavily, sweating from his exertion and the heat, and heard a strange sound behind him. He puzzled over it, then recognized it as something moving through water, shallow water.

A man appeared over him, the same man he recalled seeing before. Not an apparition then, he thought, but real and present. The man knelt at Tim's feet and smiled. "You've done well Timothy. It could not have been easy."

"How do you..."

"The pilot, Rebecca, she told me your name."

"Becks...she's alive...where...where is she...why..."

"Rest, Timothy, you need to rest. She will be here soon enough."

Tim wanted to ask more questions, but his body and mind were spent. He lost consciousness again, and did not awaken until the following dawn.

The witness sat beside the fire, and remained there through the night. He took his smudgestick from his pack, unwrapped it, and touched the end to the flames. When he had a steady column of smoke rising from it, he placed it on a piece of untanned hide in front of him, and began to sing. This time, he did not pray for a gentle passage from this world to the next, for either victim of the crash. This time, he prayed for an early end to the storm, a break in the clouds, a chance for rescue to arrive before it was too late. This time, he prayed for sun.

Day 2:
Dawn
Rebecca

Becks woke to the sound of something moving across the forest floor. Twigs snapped, pine needles rustled, then a pause. Something breathed, sniffed the air, then moved again. Her feet were uphill, her pulse was pounding in her head. She felt as though her skull was ready to crack open, then recalled that it already had.

She managed to sit up in time to see the wolves moving

toward her from three directions.

She rolled to her left, toward the pile of rubble that had once been part of her plane, and began frantically searching around the pilot's seat. Her motion momentarily stopped the pack's advance, but she knew it was a temporary reprieve.

She grew frantic, until she spotted what she was seeking. An orange plastic box, 18 inches long, six inches deep, with a large black latch on one side. It had been dislodged from its bracket under the seat and tossed backwards, wedging itself into a gap where a window had once been. She lunged for it as the wolves moved in. She pulled the box to her chest, and turned back to face the pack. She could see four of them, but assumed there were more. She yanked at the latch, spilling the contents onto her lap.

Hands shaking, she lifted the flare gun, opened its breach, and jammed a cartridge into the chamber. She had seconds before they were on her. She wasted no time thinking it over. She aimed at the nearest animal and squeezed the trigger. The flare exploded out of the barrel and slammed into the wolf's chest.

The animal made a horrible noise, a sort of prolonged scream. It spun away as the charge burned its fur and gashed its flesh. The flare ricocheted off the first animal and struck another a glancing blow. Enough to frighten it, but doing little harm.

Becks hurried to load another round, but her first volley was enough to send the pack into retreat. Nevertheless, she kept the weapon in her hand, stuffed two more cartridges into her pockets, then used the wreckage to pull herself to her feet.

She looked up through the gap in the trees and was astonished to see a brief break in the grey sky, a tiny hint of blue and sunlight, a flash of color that vanished as quickly as it appeared. But it was enough. Enough to get her moving.

Enough to give her hope.

Becks considered heading down the slope, to follow the stranger to follow him to Tim. But she needed water, and if Tim was alive, he would need it too. And food.

She rummaged around in the wreckage and located her thermal carafe, still filled with coffee. She then found the lunch she'd packed…was it the day before? Two days ago? Nothing was certain other than the need for water, and the need to find Tim. The coffee wasn't warm, but she guzzled it down all the same. It would hydrate, energize, help her focus.

While she finished the coffee she thought about Tim. And the wolves, and the man who'd materialized out of the forest then climbed a tree to speak to her. To what end? She'd gotten *herself* out of the tree, and paid for the effort with fresh bruises and a head wound. A far cry from rescue. And the wolves. The wolves would have been no threat to her, hanging up in a tree. But now they were, and they were a threat to Tim as well.

Tim. Timothy Reese Holt. Not the richest man in the world, not by a long shot. But in his world, descended from Canadian business royalty, a definite one-percenter, rich enough to have his own plane. Rich enough to hire a top-tier pilot away from a her corporate gig at an oil and gas company.

He was also kind, and decent, and respectful enough to pry her out of her self-imposed solitude. First for a coffee, then a lunch, then a series of increasingly romantic dates.

Tim, though born into wealth, had spit out the silver spoon and taken his own path. He was self-made, and self-confident. He didn't wine and dine her at the finest restaurants, though he could certainly afford it.

No, for Tim, a true romantic, everywhere they went, everything they did together, it was all imbued with something special. The ambience of a food truck at a rodeo, the salt air of a beachfront fish shack, the thrill of opening night at the theater, or the exhilaration of a album release party for the latest up-and-coming country music star.

He never tried to impress her. It was all designed to let her know who he really was, beneath the wealth and all its trappings. And it was, she knew, an effort to find out who she was. And if she was interested in more than his money.

When he'd invited her to go scuba diving with sharks off the Yucatan peninsula, she drew the line and gave a firm 'hell no.' He accepted her rejection without drama. That's when they both knew, this thing between them might have legs.

But Tim would have to wait.

Becks removed the foam packing from the flare gun case, placed her lunch inside, and headed in the direction she thought would take her to the spring. Water, for both of them. That was her priority. She had to find the spring.

She limped along and scanned the surrounding forest, stopping occasionally to listen for any sound of the wolves, looking for signs she was on the right path. On her third pause, she heard the sound of moving water, gurgling through the forest, and knew she was heading in the right direction. She was hobbled by pain, from an ankle that wouldn't quite straighten out, but she managed to keep her feet under her, and keep moving.

Timothy

Tim became aware of the world again, dragged back to consciousness by pale light, and smoke entering his nostrils, filling his lungs. He coughed, then his body convulsed as he writhed in pain. He rolled onto his back, caught a brief patch of blue sky between threatening clouds, then rolled over onto his other side, away from the smoke, trying to regain his breath without another fit of coughing.

A voice, deep baritone and melodic, spoke to him, "Good morning, Timothy. It is good to see you are still among the living."

Tim could not see him, but he assumed the voice belonged to the man who'd visited him the day before…or was it two days? "Where…," he sputtered, "where are you?"

"I am here, where I was before," the voice said from behind him.

Tim pushed against the pebbles and stiff sand of the shore and rolled over again. For the first time he saw the man as more than shape and sound. He saw his face, oval and brown, and shiny black hair under a red and black woolen cap. He wore jeans, and a dark green jacket, a large rucksack sat next to him on the gravel. He sat with his legs crossed, hands placed on his knees. He smiled at Tim. His look and tone seemed to Tim more appropriate for old friends on a fishing trip, out of synch with the situation.

"You're…First Nations…your people…are they near? Can they help me?"

"First Nations? My people…my people are not here. My people are to the south of here, to the west, the east, some far to the north. But they are not here. They have not been here for many, many years."

Speech brought more pain, but Tim felt compelled to persist. "Who…" He whispered, then caught his breath and started again, "Who are you? How…how did you…find me?"

The man shrugged and his smile grew wider, "Who? It does not matter who. How? That was easy, a plane, falling from the sky? It makes a lot of noise, especially when it… lands."

"What's…your…name?"

"My name is a name you would find difficult to pronounce. But if you need a name for me, you may call me Johnny."

"Johnny…okay…Johnny…Johnny on the spot…Johnny…I think I'm dying. Where's Becks? Is she okay?"

"Yes, Timothy, you are dying. But you are not dead yet. Although, if you keep this up, you may hurry the process along. You should rest. Help is on the way, it is a matter time."

"Time…I don't have time…I need a doctor…"

"You need a hospital," the man said with a chuckle, "one with *many* doctors. And nurses. And machines. No Timothy, you do not need a doctor, you need much more."

"You don't seem...you don't seem bothered by this…a man, dying at your feet…"

"But you are not dead, Timothy, and I am happy about this. I am happy for you, and I am happy for Rebecca who is called Becks. I prefer Rebecca, but I respect her choice. It's her name, after all, isn't it?"

"I'm cold…so cold…I…"

"Yes, the fire has gone out. Nothing but smoke and ash now. But there are a few embers buried down inside somewhere."

"Start it again…please…Johnny…I'm so cold…aren't you cold?"

"No, I'm fine, do not worry about me. Rebecca…Becks… she will revive the fire when she arrives. She shouldn't be much longer. She will bring you water, and rekindle the fire…"

"How do you know…know..."

Tim's words faded as his strength left him. He fought to keep his eyes open, to question this person, Johnny, but he lost the battle and his lids fluttered shut. He wondered, as he slipped back into darkness, what game this strange man was playing with his life.

Water, and Pain

Becks smelled the water before she saw it, but the sound had been growing louder as she made her way along the trail, the signs of the man's previous presence becoming more obvious to her as she made her way. A broken twig, a scuff in the forest floor, displaced rocks. These, and other signs, became apparent to her and she eventually found herself on a game trail leading roughly north.

She couldn't describe the smell of the stream, but she knew it somehow. That it was fast-flowing and voluminous was evident by the sound. But the smell, having left behind the acrid smells of the crash site, the fresh scent of a stream, *clean* and *sweet* in the otherwise dank and musty forest. When the path rounded a chest-high boulder, she found the stream rushing at her feet, cascading over rocks and ledges, clear and fast, headed down the gully toward the lake.

She fell to her knees and plunged her hands into the frigid water, was about to drink, then saw the filth on her hands and arms. She scooped up fine gravel and silt from a small eddy and scrubbed away the blood and grime, then scooped the water again and gulped it down. She splashed it on her face, over her hair, felt its chill rolling under her collar and down her back.

She shivered, gave a smile at this small wonder, the pleasure of the cold, then drank more, drank until she was full and drank more. She knew the indulgence of drinking too much too fast could cause water intoxication, and compound her problems, even kill her. She didn't care. She'd rather risk it than end up thirsty again by the time she located Tim. Whatever water she could carry, it would be for him.

If Tim were unable to move, she would need her strength for both of them. She rinsed and filled her thermos, then sat beside the torrent and ate the food she'd carried from the crash. While she ate, she contemplated her surroundings, assessing the area as she had been taught during her survival training.

Were there sources of food? The lake, for certain, but could she catch anything there? As for game, the wolves were evidence of the presence of other animals. They had to eat too, and they'd looked plenty healthy to her. If she and Tim were stranded more than a few days, she'd have to figure something out, some way to trap or fish or gather.

She let out a grim laugh, "Girl," she said aloud, "you went from the Jet Age to the Stone Age in a single day. Ain't that something?"

She checked her watch and was surprised to see it was past noon. The day was escaping her, and she wondered if the wound in her head was more than skin deep.

She filled the plastic box with water, topped off her thermos, gathered her strength, and began the walk back the way she'd come, back toward the crash. Toward Tim.

Initially, the return trip was uphill, and slippery, and took longer than she expected. By the time she made it back to her original starting point, it was after 3pm. Sunset, at her current latitude and time of year, would not be far off. Based on what the man in the tree had told her, she was an hour's walk from Tim, at least. Likely more, given the poor pace she was keeping.

She sat on the forest floor, near the remains of the fire, near where the man had been when she first saw him. She drank a little water, examined her ankle, then gingerly touched the wound on her head. After having washed it by the stream, her scalp didn't feel quite as bad, but her hands came away bloodied.

"It's just the water," she assured herself, "makes it look worse. A little blood goes a long way. Now get on up, and get moving."

She pushed herself to her feet. On her first step, her injured ankle twisted hard to the side. Searing pain shot up through her leg, sending her crashing back down, grinding her face into the thick layer of twigs and pine needles and decay.

She rolled onto her back, stared up at the broken trees and the dimming sky. Her emotions gathered, formed a growing wave, and threatened to overwhelm her. She screamed her rage into the sky, sent it flying with her fear and frustration, then shook her head to clear her mind.

She heard her father's voice, from her childhood, admonishing her when she'd once pitched a fit over some perceived affront, or petty grievance, at the park near their home. She was nine when he said, "Not now kiddo, not here, save your tantrums for your bedroom, nobody here wants to hear it."

He hadn't dismissed her feelings, he'd simply told her to manage them. The lesson was lost on her then, but she'd grown to understand it, to understand him. He was not cruel or unkind. But he expected her to learn life's harder lessons when she was young, in hopes of avoiding greater pain later in life. It's possible, she thought, he always knew she'd end up in the military, like him, where such lessons would serve her well.

Lessons which she knew had prepared her for the crisis she now faced.

The trees, after all, didn't give a damn about her problems. Any more than the wolves or the birds and anything else lurking about. Except, maybe, the man who'd left her in the tree to find her own way down. He seemed to care, and yet, he didn't seem eager to offer up more than words of encouragement.

Becks rolled over onto all fours and scanned the forest floor. A few yards away she spotted what she needed - a branch, long enough and strong enough to help her get to her feet again. She crawled to the branch, rose up on her knees and braced herself. She took a deep breath, pulled herself up, and tried to keep her weight off her damaged ankle. She managed to stand and found herself looking down the slope. She loosened her belt and slipped it through the thermos handle, attaching it to one hip, then the box at the other, making herself into a collection of found objects, dangling and rattling.

"At least it's all down hill from here," she said, and began to move, anxious to find Tim before she ran out of daylight. The thought of him injured, suffering, helpless. It terrified her and spurred her on, as did the thought of herself being injured and alone in the dark forest. She quickened her pace as best she could.

Evening, and a Dying Man
Tim

Tim slept through most of the day, but it was a twilight sleep, tormented by pain, bothered by strange dreams; dreams of arguments, dreams of laughter, dreams of a life he was slowly losing.

He was awakened by a scream in the distance.

He shivered uncontrollably, his body heat gone, hypothermia tightening its grip. He knew the stages, and found himself longing for that point where he would no longer feel the cold, the penultimate stage of the process. A gentle kind of passing, albeit a terrible way to die.

He looked at Johnny, still seated where he'd been earlier in the day. Johnny's eyes were closed, but he opened them at the sound of Tim's stirring.

"Ah," he said, smiling, "you're still live! This is good."

Tim's speech was already difficult, but his worsening

condition caused him to begin slurring his words, "I heard… a scream…someone…"

"You heard her? That is very good. That is Rebecca, who you call Becks. She is finally on her way here."

Tim's heart raced. Why would Becks be screaming? And why had she stopped screaming? She'd been in the nose of the plane, she must be injured, but if she was on the move…

"Why…why screaming?"

Johnny let out a huff and shook his head, "Why?" he repeated. "Why is something you will have to ask her. But I would think she may find all of this more than a little frustrating. Wouldn't you? It could be enough to make anyone scream. But not you, of course. You're in no condition to scream."

Cold tears rolled across Tim's nose and cheeks, "I don't… understand…"

"Of course you don't, not now. You're in the thick of it, aren't you? But if you find your way through this, you will understand, in time. But that is not important today. Today, all that matters is you are alive, and someone, apparently someone you care about and cares about you, that someone will be here soon. She will help you, you will complete your journey. This is exciting. One way or another, you will finish this adventure together. Tell me, what is Rebecca to you? A friend, your wife, are you romantic?"

"You make…no sense…"

"Me? I am not important, not in that way. There's no need to be. But tell me, please, I am curious. Tell me about Rebecca, and you."

Tim stared at the man, desperate, angry, then resigned. What else was there to do, he thought. This man seated in front of Tim was at least a distraction from his suffering. Tim inhaled as much as he could, slowly, to avoid a fit of coughing and convulsing. As he did so, his shivers lessened, and the deep chill seemed to shift into a spreading warmth.

"Becks…I love her…was going to propose…Fairbanks… romantic…"

"Ah, this is the start of a good story. Do you think she will say yes?"

Tim had been nervous about proposing to Becks, frightened by the prospect. He had imagined what would happen if she said no. She would quit her job as his pilot. She'd have no trouble finding work, and he wouldn't stand in her way. She'd move on to fly someone else's plane, or take some other role, far away from him. She'd have her share of suiters, no doubt, and could pick from among them as she liked.

He would go on as he had before. Alone, lonely, but this time with little interest in finding a new relationship. Becks was willful, independent, and free in every sense. The very traits that attracted him were the ones that scared him. *She* didn't need him in order to be happy, but *he* could not imagine being happy again, without her.

At length he replied, "I don't know."

"You can't know, but how do you feel? Do you feel…"

Tim felt anger welling up again, and managed to ask, while gasping for air, "Why do you care?"

"Be careful, Timothy, you don't want to strain yourself," Johnny said, his tone flat, matter-of-fact. "She is not far away, you may want to be awake, in case she is looking for you in the darkness. There is no moon tonight, and you might want to ask her when you see her, in case…"

"Why…do…you…care?"

Johnny raised a hand to his face, stroked his chin as if stroking an imaginary beard, "The truth, Timothy, is I do not care. Not in the way your question implies. You live, you die, it changes nothing for me. But two people in love? This is a story worth hearing, don't you agree? In this, I do have an interest, I do care. What a person does with the life they have, this is of interest to me. You, her, the love you feel for her. These are a kind of hope, an aspiration, for both of you. If she loves you, it would be nice if she said yes, wouldn't it? But what does your heart tell you?"

"I don't understand."

"Understanding," Johnny said, smiling, with a soft laugh, "is overrated."

Tim closed his eyes, let his mind wander, thought about the things he and Becks had experienced in the time they'd had together. There had been disagreements, of course, but they'd always found their way back to a place of peace and understanding. It was more than compatibility, it was more than love. It was as if they were meant to find each other, and yet completely unlikely. They were each the part they never knew they'd been missing.

"She'll say yes," he whispered, then opened his eyes. The daylight had grown dim, the grey sky darkened. He'd slept again, with no way of knowing how long.

And Johnny was gone.

Farewell, Traveler

Becks

Once Timothy passed out again, Johnny rose and made his way up the slope, leaving the dying man near the ashes of the fire, curious to learn of the progress Rebecca had made. He knew she would be on her way, especially after speaking with Timothy. Young lovers, young to him anyway, would go to great lengths for one another. This was a truth he knew well.

Unless she didn't love him, in which case she could easily have encamped near the wreckage, leaving her passenger to his fait. But Johnny did not give this notion serious consideration. The woman had made it clear on their first meeting; Timothy mattered to her.

As he considered these two people, dropped into the world by whatever chance occurrence had destroyed their plane, a thought came to him, clear like a ringing bell. What if she... but no, he shooed the idea away, a pesky fly of speculation not worthy of his time. Unless...

He heard her approach before he saw her. He stopped, leaned against a tree, and waited. It was their mutual good fortune to encounter one another at a point where the underbrush cleared and the forest was not quite as dark. He would get a proper measure of her condition.

Becks, though, was focused more on staying upright than on what lay ahead. She tried to keep a straight path down the slope. She kept her eyes grounded, avoiding another fall. There had been two so far, each painful. The process of getting back to her feet was sapping her strength. It was no surprise that she didn't see the man until she was nearly stepping on his toes, after pushing her way through a thick patch of low bushes.

"You are making good progress, Rebecca," the man said.

His voice brought her up short, her eyes shot to his face, saw his slight smile, and she nearly lost her footing again.

"What the...," she started, but he cut her off.

"Careful now, you don't want to break the other ankle, do you?"

Her frustration was already near her boiling point. This person, she thought, with his nonchalance, he was certain to push her over it. She couldn't stop herself from snapping at him, "Where did you come from? Where's Tim? What..."

The man swung his arm down the slope and pointed, "I came from the island, I was with Tim, he is still alive, but he is struggling. He fell asleep, again, so I thought I'd come to see how you were doing. You seem well equipped. You have water for him?"

"The fact you find this amusing is not lost on me. Who the hell are you? Are you having fun, hanging around, watching us die out here? Where did you come from? Why…"

"Let's begin with the easiest answer," he said, cutting her off again. "As I told your kîhithaw, you may call me Johnny. It pains me that you think I enjoy your suffering. I give you my word, I do not enjoy it. But seeing you on your feet, making your way to Timothy, this makes me happy. Why wouldn't it? You are alive, you are still on your journey, and you may reach your destination, your next one, in time. *Of course* this makes me happy. It is a beautiful thing, the human spirit, the will to live, to fight for life. Don't you agree?"

Becks wondered for a moment if this man, Johnny, was as vexing to Tim as he was to her. "What's a kee-hee-thaw? I don't know your language, I need…"

"It is not my language, it is a word of the Cree. I like it. It has a sound like that which it signifies, I think, which is always good for a word. You might say 'boyfriend' in your language."

"Tim…"

"Has been kind enough to share a little of his story with me. I wish he could have shared more. And I wish you and I had time to speak a little of your life. I think you've had an interesting life. It would be enjoyable to hear your thoughts about the path you have walked. But your clock is ticking, and my clock is ticking, and Tim's clock is ticking, each with its own rhythm and pace. His faster than yours, faster than mine…"

"Time? Are you speaking in riddles? Time, I don't have time for you. How far away is he? Can I make it before dark?"

"All things we do not understand are riddles, but time is something we make ourselves, easy enough to understand.

He is not far, you are not far. When you reach the water's edge, look for my footprints, they will lead you into the shallows, and out again."

Johnny pushed away from the tree and started up the ridge. He raised a hand as if to place it on Becks' shoulder, then lowered it to his side. "The water is cold," he said, "you will need fire. There are ashes over embers you can breathe into life. Be patient, then build it big, as large as you can, and do not mind the smoke."

As he walked away from her, Becks felt a strange sense of panic, as if she was losing someone. And yet, he'd been of no help, none at all. And still, she didn't want him to leave.

She felt tears welling up in her eyes, felt her fear and desperation gripping her chest, closing her throat, "Where are you going?" Why won't you help us?"

Johnny looked over his shoulder, his smile faded to a frown, "But I have helped you. I have done all I can do. I am not a doctor. I can't carry you to the nearest village. I have no food, no medicine. But I have done what I am able, as best I can. This trouble is your trouble, not mine. And yet I have been here, with you, for as long as I can. But our time together is over. Go, be with Timothy, build a great fire. If you survive the night, you will see what tomorrow brings, and your journey may end, or it may begin again. This is not up to me. I have done all I can. Goodbye Rebecca who is called Becks."

Johnny turned away from her and continued on his way.

"No!" she cried. Her emotions had broken through her last line of defense, "Don't leave us out here," she shouted. "Don't leave me out here! What do I do if Tim dies? I don't want to be alone out here!"

Johnny stopped walking but did not turn around. He raised his hand, pointed one finger at the sky, "You will build a fire," he said, then pointed a second finger to the sky, "and you will survive the night. Nothing beyond that can be know." He dropped his hand, and continued his slow march up the slope, away from her, pushing his way into the underbrush.

Becks leaned against her crutch and shouted after him, "Then to hell with you old man! To hell with you!"

She stared at the low branches until they stopped moving, then turned and started down the slope again. Each step closer to Tim, further away from Johnny, and deeper into the unknown.

By the time she arrived at the shore of the lake, the light had nearly gone, and with it, much of her strength. She saw the remains of the passenger cabin partially submerged, and beyond it an island, Tim's island. She looked along the near bank and spotted an area that had been disturbed, a muddy patch of small ridges and indentations - footprints.

She lunged into the water, shouting, "Tim, Tim, I'm here. Where are you?"

She lost her footing and fell into the lake, gulping in fuel-laced water, soaking herself in the frigid chill. She came up sputtering, gasping for air. She tried to stand, and fell again. She shoved her branch-crutch aside, sending it drifting away, and swam toward the island, pulling with her arms as she kept her eyes on the nearing shore. Before she reached him, she saw him, lying on his side, facing away from her, and his legs at a horrifying angle to his body. She could see the remains of a large fire spread out a few feet from him.

When she felt a gravel shore beneath her, she crawled out of the water toward him. When she reached him, she was careful not to touch his legs, but a cursory examination revealed at least one open fracture. She looked at his face, pale, gaunt, muddied and bloodied, and for a moment thought she was too late. She placed a hand on his shoulder, then two fingers on his neck. When she didn't feel a pulse, she blew on her fingers to warm them, then pressed again, harder this time, and felt the faintest of throbs. It was weak, she held her fingers in place to make certain, then saw a tiny bubble escape his nostril, an exhale. 'Alive,' she thought, her heart pounding, 'he's alive.'

"Tim," she said quietly, "Timmy love, it's me, I'm here. Timmy can you hear me?"

When he did not respond, she began to cry, the stress taking over, "Wake up love. Please, wake up. Timmy, I need you, please..."

His eyes fluttered, opened slightly, and his mouth moved, but she couldn't hear what he said. She leaned in close, her ear touching his lips, "Becks," she heard him say, "Becks... I'm dying."

Adrenalin surged through her body. She pulled her hand away from him, sat up, and barked at him like a drill sergeant, "No! No sir, not on my watch you're not."

She swiped the tears away from her face and looked around. Should couldn't see any burning embers glowing in the dim light that was quickly turning to darkness. She threw her hands into the ash, finding a bed of coals the only way she could, by burning her fingers on them.

She felt around the edges of the fire, grabbing any small twigs from the fire's periphery, and piled them onto the heat. She blew into the coals she had exposed, but try as she might she couldn't coax enough flame to set the twigs alight.

She turned to the wreckage in the water and realized a portion of the plane's tail was still attached to the cabin. She dragged herself across the rocky beach, into the water, and swam toward the hulking mass.

She pulled herself around the side and into the end. She pushed and pulled tangled wires and debris out of her way and found what she was looking for; a set of small storage compartments adjacent to the place where the bathroom had been. She pried it open. Her spirits were buoyed by what what was inside. Amongst the various items, most of them useless to her, she found a first aid kit and, as she had hoped, a pile of small blankets, sealed in plastic, all of which fell out of the compartment and floated around her.

She grabbed as many as she could, tucked the first aid kit under her arm, and made her way out of the wreck, back into open water. She threw the kit and the blankets onto the shore, then went back into the plane. She grabbed the remaining blankets and left the cabin. She threw them onto the island with the others, then crawled her way back to Tim, dragging the first aid kit with her.

She opened the plastic box, tossing aside the useless adhesive bandages and antibiotic ointment pouches until she located what she wanted: alcohol wipes, and a sealed pack of cotton balls. She tore open the plastic with her teeth, then opened the alcohol wipes and stuff the moist papers into the bag with the cotton balls.

She squeezed and shook the bag, transferring some of the alcohol to the cotton, "Almost there love," she said. "We'll have a fire in no time, then blankets. We'll get warmed up in no time, you'll see. Hang in there Timmy, hang in there..."

She removed most of the twigs she'd piled onto the embers, dumped the cotton and alcohol mass in their place, then leaned over and blew gently on the embers, watching the glow increased with every breath.

She was beginning to feel dizzy from the effort when suddenly a blue-orange flame, small but strong, erupted only inches from her nose. She sat back on her knees, ignoring the pain from her ankle. She carefully placed twigs on the flame, allowing each to catch before adding more, trying not to snuff out their only hope of survival.

"Build a fire," she said, "and live through the night. That's the plan Timmy. You with me? That's the plan. Build a big-ass fire and we live. That's the plan."

She continued building the fire, adding larger twigs and branches she gathered from around her, then finally tossing a log, a few inches thick and wider than the entire fire, onto the flames. She watched it catch, and smiled, knowing she had something sustainable. She dragged other chunks of wood onto the fire, until she had a healthy blaze, flames three to four feet tall, crackling away.

It was then, with waves of warmth washing over her, she realized how cold she had become - her body heat had been maintained by her activity. The moment she stopped, she began to cool down, and quickly.

She crawled around the beach, gathering the plastic-wrapped blankets, eight in all.

"Blanket's Timmy," she said. "I'm gonna wrap you up like a burrito, get you warmed up and toasty."

She looked at his face and despite the warm glow of the fire he was pale and drawn under the muck and mess all over him. She tore open the bags and wrapped him in four of the blankets, then wrapped one around her upper body, tying it in front of her so she could continue moving around, gathering wood until she had a pile close to Tim and the fire.

Once again, after she stopped moving, she felt the cold set in.

"Okay big boy, I'm coming in," she said, "but don't get any ideas, no hank-panky tonight mister."

She lay down behind him, draping one leg over his hips, and pulled herself as close to his body as she could get. She layered the remaining blankets over both of them, then wrapped her arm around his chest. "I bet this would hurt like hell if you were awake," she said, then tucked her elbow under her head, and nestled her nose into the nape of his neck, filling her nostrils with the smell of him, and the mud and the blood. But mostly him.

She felt exhaustion winning the day, the heat of the fire bathing them both, the heat of her body flowing to him, and at last, she began to fall asleep. As she was drifting off, she heard Tim speak, but couldn't understand him. She propped herself up and leaned over him.

"It's okay love, I'm here, right here, it's okay."

His eyes were closed, but he was smiling, a little, when he whispered, as if from deep within a dream, "Becks...," he said, "Becks...will you...marry me...Becks...marry me..."

When he fell quiet again, back into his silent delirium, she laid back down against him, again pulling herself close to him, and replied, whispering in his ear, "Such a romantic..." before drifting off to sleep.

After

Tim found the Adirondack chairs around the fire pit to his liking. Large, comfortable, the perfect angled seat backs for relaxing, wide arms to rest a drink. The fire was large and threw ample warmth at him, as did the glass of red wine in his hand. It felt as though he'd been waiting all night for Becks. He worried they might be late. As he had the thought, he struggled to recall where they were going that night. Some sort of party, a charity event. It didn't matter, he was dressed for going out and it was strange she was taking so long. He stood, sipped his wine, then reached into his jacket pocket. He reassured himself the box, the one holding the ring, the ring his mother had passed to him, was till there waiting, like him, for Becks.

He turned his back to the fire, looked down the lawn, blue and black under the gibbous moon, tendrils of firelight cast against the dark. Behind him he heard a familiar sound, the heavy door sliding open. But there was something about Becks' footsteps on the flagstone patio...was she...barefoot?

He smiled and turned around to face her, ready to give due praise to whatever beautiful dress she had chosen for the evening. She didn't care if he liked what she wore, but he always did. Her taste was that good. Exceptional, her friends, their family, often said.

This time, though, she had outdone herself. "Becks," he said, laughing, swinging his arms wide, fast enough to spill his drink, "it took you all day to come up with this? Sweat pants and my hockey jersey? I take it we're staying in?"

"Yeah," she said, taking his glass from his hand, and placing it on the stone knee wall behind him. "Who needs a night out when we could have a night right here?"

She stared into the night, as he had, then looked up at the moon shining above, stars twinkling from billions of miles away. She turned to face him and placed a hand on his chest, directly above the pocket holding the small box.

"I have something to tell you," she said, "and I didn't want to wait until tomorrow."

"Funny," he replied, "I have something to ask you, and I don't want it to wait. Guess that means…"

"You go first," she said, gently patting her hand against his chest, over his heart.

"No m'am, I'm a gentleman. Ladies first, always."

She rolled her eyes, turned her head a little, to catch another glimpse of the moon, "Okay, " she said, "lady's first."

She looked into his eyes and felt as if she could see his soul looking back at her. She took a deep breath, and on her exhale said, soft as the wind in summer, "I'm pregnant. You're gonna be a daddy."

Tim took her hand from his chest, held it, and took a half step back, before moving closer to her again. He was overwhelmed, felt tears forming, "Becks," he said, "I thought we couldn't."

"Me too," she said. "I guess the doctors were wrong. Or

something, I don't know, clicked into place." She reached up and wiped her thumb across his cheek, gathered a few of his tears, then place her thumb against her lips, smiling up at him. "You're taking it well, I see."

"It's…I…wow, Becks, yeah, I'm…I dreamed of a family with you, one day, but it was never, you know, it didn't have to happen, it wasn't a requirement, or anything, but, you and me and baby makes three, how cool is that? But….are you okay? How do you feel about this? I mean…your career…"

She looked at the night sky again, where movement above held her gaze. A tiny light passed overhead. A satellite? Space station? A distant plane, far removed for their patch of earth? She couldn't say, but she watched until it was gone, then turned her attention back to Tim.

"I'm okay," she said. "I'm good. I'm, yeah, I'm great. I'm ready for a change. Right here, now, this…I love you, and this baby, I mean, it's a change all right. I think I'll be happy on the ground, for a while."

She pulled her sleeve over her hand and wiped more tears from Tim's face, "Will you stop already? You're gonna make me cry, and I don't like to cry. It'll mess up my makeup."

"You're not wearing makeup."

"A technicality, don't argue."

Tim laughed and looked into her eyes, but said nothing.

"I hear those gears grinding up there mister. What did you want to tell me? Your turn, talk to me."

He reached into his pocket, and pulled out the box. "Well, um, this may not the best timing," he said. He tapped his free hand on his leg, "You know I can't really bend the knee and all, but, you know, I hope that's okay, because, I was wondering if, maybe, if you're so inclined, Becks…will you marry me?"

He opened the box, presenting the ring to her.

She looked at the ring, tiny and sparkling like the light

she'd watched glide over them. She knew it had been passed through generations, from a time before his family had gained their wealth, its value entirely sentimental. She slipped a single finger over the small stone, feeling its edges, the mounting, the band. She smiled up at him, closed the box, wrapped her hand around it, placed her other hand back over his heart.

A loud pop sounded from a burning log. They were startled from their moment, instinctively wrapping their arms around each other, pulling each other close, turning their gaze to the fire together.

Flames curled up, carrying glowing embers with them. Tiny orange lights, spiraling up into the darkness, disappearing as quickly as they'd appeared.

Becks marveled at their transient beauty, then looked up at Tim, his face aglow, warm and smiling, the essence of calm, a man at peace.

The man she loved.

"Kiss me," she said.

And he did.

Justus

OUR FAITH CAN MOVE
MOUNTAINS.
BE STILL AND KNOW
GOD IS MY REFUGE.
GOD IS THE STRENGTH
OF MY HEART

Justice, like vengeance, can take many forms. Sometimes, the two can become confused with one another, especially in a place with a history steeped in secrets and lies.

Morganville, Georgia, a small town ninety minutes east of Atlanta. Old South, old money, old stories. A journalism student at the University of Georgia, I'd been recruited to visit places like Morganville and interview elderly locals, gathering up oral histories before the people who carried them died, and the stories were lost forever. It could be a boring gig, but occasionally I came across a doozy of a tale.

That's what happened in Morganville. I look back on that afternoon as a turning point. It changed the way I approached my job, and my life, which led to a better job, and eventually a career in journalism. But back then, I was a kid with a tape recorded, a truck with no AC, and a long hot summer ahead of me.

I took Athens Highway south toward Morganville, with plans to do some research at the local library, after a stop in Apalachee for breakfast. Biscuits and gravy with grits and a bottomless glass of the sweetest ice tea ever brewed.

Esther's Soul Food was the best food around, and I never missed a chance to stop in for a bite. It was a place out of time, perfectly maintained, sandwiched between a one-pump gas station and a falling-down hardware store. People lined up to eat there for lunch and supper.

The current owner was Esther's granddaughter, Annie. She ran the place the same way her mother, and her grandmother, had run it. Everyone was welcome, including pasty-white me. Maybe it helped her son was my best friend and roommate. I liked to think that didn't matter. She was good people and good to me, that's all I knew.

While I sat at the counter eating breakfast, she told me about 'old man Gentry' and the highway marker put up in his name after he died.

"Do yourself a favor," she said, "skip the Morganville library. Take a spin down Lower Apalachee road, it'll swing you onto Route 12, then into the backside of Morganville."

"Why would I wanna do that Miss Annie?"

"Because I said so," she said, feigning insult. Then she smiled, "There's a historical marker by the road, right on the town line. You keep your eyes peeled and you stop and give it a read. If it grabs your interest, you go on into town and search out old man Barnsley at Morganville Mercantile, I'll write the address down. He's old as Methuselah. If I know him, he'll be perched in his store, hoping for someone like you to come along and darken his doorstep. He doesn't get much business these days, he's got plenty of time to chat you up. And he does like to talk, once you get him going."

"You think he's got a story worth hearing?"

"If he doesn't, you come back here for supper and your meal is on the house."

"And if he does..."

"You come back here all the same and show me some appreciation. Either way, I'll make sure we don't run out of chicken before you get here."

"It's a deal," I said, "I'll see you soon."

I paid and left with a tall paper cup of tea for the road. Between the sugar and the caffeine I was feeling pretty good. I hooked a right onto Lower Apalachee and was on my way. A mile or so after turning onto Route 12, which had a sign labelling it as "Peter Gentry Parkway," I came to the marker.

It was a big bronze-looking plaque bolted to a rusty pole. I eased onto the gravel shoulder and got out, surveyed the corn fields bordering the road to the west and east, ready for harvest, then walked over to the marker for a closer look.

At first it didn't seem like much. 'Peter William Gentry died on this spot...blah blah blah...Pillar of the community... blah blah..." boring stuff until I got to the last line.

That's the line that hooked me.

'Vengeance is Mine.'

It was followed by 'Deuteronomy 32:35.' It was not raised in relief like the main passage, but painted neatly in one line along the bottom. It was obvious someone had added it to the plaque. The gold paint was losing the fight against the elements, but was in better shape than the rest of the lettering.

"That is interesting," I said aloud, then jumped into my truck and drove on.

The building I came to, with a sign that read 'Morganville Mercantile,' looked more like a home than a business. A gravel lot in front, peeling white paint over warped clapboard siding, with black-trimmed windows and a rattling screen in front of a single wooden front door, also black. The inner door was held open by a chunk of granite.

The screen door opened with a screech. Hinges so loose, I worried it would come off in my hands. Inside, wide-planked floors under a layer of dust, narrow aisles between bins and tables loaded with everything from canning supplies to hand tools, to saltwater taffy and wind-up toys. It was as much a museum as a retail operation.

A potbellied stove sat cold at the rear of the shop, flanked by two tattered armchairs, one occupied by an elderly white man, dressed for church, or dinner, or anyplace but there. Black leather shoes, dark brown trousers, pressed white shirt, suspenders, and a bowtie to top it all off. A fan spun languidly overhead, another on the floor oscillated up at him.

The bricks behind the stove were covered with Bible quotes painted in gold. The style was immediately familiar.

"You must be that boy outta Athens," he said.

"Yes sir, Thomas Wright, I'm with…"

"Annie called about you," he interrupted, "said you was workin' for the radio station, recordin' old folks tellin' stories."

"I work for the Southern History Center," I replied. "Our project is funded from the public radio budget, but I don't work for…"

"Them's that payin' ya is them's ya work for, in my book."

"I won't argue with your logic Mister Barnsley."

I felt as though the story had already begun, and I was missing it. I raised my tape recorder. "Mind if I have a seat and turn this gizmo on?"

"That's what you're here for, ain't it?"

"Yes sir."

"Annie said you's polite as the day is long. Go 'head on, have a seat."

He waved his hand at the chair facing him. I placed the recorder on the stove and started the same as I always did. "Rolling tape…this is a recording for the Rural Voices project of the Southern History Center, June third, 1978. Subject James Lee Barnsley, age…"

"Eighty-nine last month, May fourteen."

"…age 89, Morganville, Georgia. Mister Barnsley, I understand you have a story to share regarding Mister Peter Gentry and his role in the history of Morganville."

"You betchya I do," he said "You done seen that marker they put up I reckon. Always strange ta me, namin' a road after a man what died on it, 'specially how…well, yeah, I can tell y'all 'bout it."

"Great, where would you like to begin?"

"I reckon I'd be wise to start at the start, dontcha think?"

"Yes sir, I do agree."

"Well awright then, let's get to it." The old man licked his lips, "Mister Peter Gentry," he said, skewing his face as if he'd just bitten into a lime. "He come from a long line a Gentrys. You know them Gentry's, they was three brothers back in the war, when Sherman marched through here with his army. Them Gentry's the ones what talked that bastard outta burnin' the whole place down, like he done Atlanta. All them big fancy houses down First Street, they owe they lives to the Gentry kin."

"I read about that in my history class. We did a section on the Civil War. He had no children, no surviving relatives?" I asked.

"Civil War? Is that what they call it now?"

"What do you call it?"

He leaned forward in his chair and glared at me, "The war of northern aggression," he said, anger spilling out.

"But didn't the South fire the first shot, Fort Sumter…"

"You keep your history, I'll keep mine. But you didn't come here 'bout that. You come here about Gentry, so let's stick to it. Long's there's been a Morganville, there's been a Gentry livin' in it, 'least 'til the old man died. He was the last of them folks ever to grace our presence."

"He never had children?"

"He ain't never got married, if that's what you're askin'."

"What about siblings?"

"Outlived his baby sister. He was the last, here or anywheres, far as I know."

"Thank you for clarifying."

"If you gonna keep askin' me questions we might be here a spell."

"I'll try to keep it to a minimum," I said.

"That'd be nice," he said, then continued. "After he r'tired from doin' not much a nuthin', he took to pushin' his bicycle 'long the road, the one you come in on, pickin' up soda bottles.

"Soda bottles…"

"They's worth a nickel apiece them days. I don't know why he done it, he ain't need no money. 'It's like pickin' up cash off the road,' he says to me. He brung his booty into my store for redeemin' so I guess he as doin' ok by it."

"Maybe he liked the exercise."

"Anything's possible. He kep' a old burlap sack hung over his handlebars an' just dropped them nickels right in, purty as you please."

"About now's when most folks will tell ya all about them Gentrys and what fine upstandin' citizens they was an how ever'body loved that family. You can read that in a book too if'n you want. Maybe it's true, but if you want all the truth, you gotta know 'bout Frank Wilson, may he rest in peace."

"Frank Wilson…a Gentry family friend?"

"Not hardly. I 'spose he had somethin' to do with that sign being up on that road, that's for sure. Back in the day, Frank had what folks round here called a big-ass pit bull, but that beast weren't no pit bull."

"Excuse me. Frank Wilson…a pit bull…what's this got to do with Gentry?"

"That is the story I'm tryin' to tell you. A little dose of patience might be useful."

"Yes sir, patience, got it."

"Alrighty then. The dog, it weren't no pit bull. It were okay with Frank if folks believed as such. If folks knew that dog were a Press-a-Canary-oh dog…dang that's hard to say…they'd a never a let him fight it. But I'm gettin' ahead of myself. I wouldn't a know'd what it was neither, if Frank hadn't a told me. He never would tell me where it come from, some kinda secret of his."

I felt like I was falling down the rabbit hole. "He fought the dog…"

"Fightin' dogs wasn't always illegal 'round here. That dog

of Frank's had plenty a work. Made a sorta livin' for Frank, that dog did. Frank bought him a big 'ol leather collar from my store, had a brass plate on it you could send off to git writ on. When I told him he done spelt Justice wrong on his slip, Frank sorta smiled and said 'It's just him and me agin' the world, so it's Justus, if ya please.'"

"Interesting…"

"Justus were a momma's nightmare. But to understand that dog, you gotta understand Frank, and what happen'd to him. Ya see, Frank was Morganville's most feared drunk. Not 'cuz a his binges, though he had his share, and not 'cuz he was ugly as sin and big as a truck, though he damn sure was both."

"Big man, big dog, booze, quite the recipe."

"You tellin' me. Frank, he had hisself whatcha call a hair trigger. You so much as look at him sidewise and he'd be on ya lickity split. He weren't never like that with me, but I ain't never give him no cause to be. We had us a right cordial relationship, me an' Frank. After what happened to him, I didn't never blame him for nothin' he did."

"Frank was your friend, not Peter Gentry's. Did they know each other?"

"I'm gettin' there. Listen, you want the short version, it won't make near as much sense. Now Frank's momma was a good lookin' woman, I tell you what, and she had her some money too. She had her a fillin' station and auto-re-pair shop down the road a piece. Didn't never give her no standin' with folks 'round Morganville, an' her hell-raisin' didn't help. She lived her life as she pleased. I thought she was a hoot and a fine dancer to boot."

"You were friendly with Frank's mother. How did Frank feel about that?"

"Friendly? I reckon you could call it that, sure. Frank didn't have no say in it, he weren't around yet when I met his momma, if you know what I mean."

"No, I'm not sure…"

"Her wild side's what got her killed. She was haulin' ass down Highway 24 on her motorbike, run smack-dab into a loggin' truck. Driver said he never seen her comin'. Poor gal ain't stood a chance."

The old man fell silent. The hint of tears glittered in his eyes. He swiped at his face and continued.

"Suzy left everthin' to Frank. He moved in with his grandaddy up in Apalachee. That ol' cuss run that station to nuthin and spent every penny of Suzy's, of Frank's, money on drinkin', curousin', and whatever old men git up to when they come by easy money."

"What about Frank's father? Was he a local…"

"Well, Frank's daddy was the sixty-four dollar question 'round town for years. Still is, if anybody's still askin'."

"A mystery then."

"You might say. Another thing Frank got from his momma was his looks. He was a fine lookin' young man, until he weren't no more. People kinda forgot Frank weren't ugly 'til 'bout ninth grade. But it weren't his fault he got ugly."

"Wait, what do you mean got ugly?"

"Hush now and listen, you'll catch up soon enough."

"Okay…"

"His first day in high school, most kids didn't know him much on account of his goin' to school up in Apalachee. But everybody was going to the same high school by then. Frank, he made a few in-dee-screet remarks to a purty young gal name'a Judy Gentry. That didn't sit too good with her big brother. He come home from college, same one as you, soon's he got word. But he weren't no youngin' like you, he was a full grow'd man then, I'd say."

"A non-traditional student."

"I don't know what that is. He come home from college

one Friday and he was waitin' outside that school for the bell to ring. He saw Frank and lit into him like a banshee from Hell. He liked to kill him, probably woulda if the principal hadn't a come along. All them other kids, they stood thar an' watched, cheered it on, most of 'em."

The old man paused again. I saw the tears return to his eyes. As before, he swiped them away before they could fall.

"Y'all know that boy's name was Peter. He got hiself back up 'er to Athens quick as lightnin', an' Frank got hiself three weeks in the hospital. They done what they could for him, but we ain't had no plastic surgeons, 'round here in them days. Frank come outta there and his looks done gone from special good to special bad. He got hiself a disposition to match too, that's for sure."

"Three weeks, from a fistfight?"

"I ain't said nothin' 'bout a fist fight. Gentry took after Frank with baseball bat, until he broke it and started kickin' him. I went up there to the hospital and set a spell most days…rough times, seein' that boy hurtin' like the devil. He didn't talk on account of the wires in his jaw, but soon as they come out he looked me dead in the eyes and says, 'I ain't never gonna let nothin' like that happen to me ever again.' I could tell by the way he done said it, he was gonna keep that promise."

"Was Peter Gentry charged?"

"Charged? For beatin' a boy from Apalachee? Things were different, a boy from Apalachee, talkin' up a gal from Morganville, he could a been sweet as Esther's tea to that gal and he woulda still got a whoopin'. Anyhow, then on, anybody'd wrong Frank, he'd have his vengeance. Kinda made me proud, I know it shouldn'ta, but it did, made me proud to see him stand up like that. But he ain't never got no payback for that first beatin'. Not before he was dead, nohow."

"Gentry got away with brutalizing Frank Wilson."

"He got away with it for a time. But the Lord says 'their foot shall slide in due time; the day of their calamity shall be at hand.' Boy was it ever for ol' man Gentry, I tell you what."

"It were a right fine day, bright and clear, when it happened. The leaves gone all glorious reds 'n golds, ragin' heat of summer turned to cooler days, perfect for sittin' in the garden or takin' long walks, things like that."

I envisioned Frank Wilson running Peter Gentry over with his car, exacting his revenge. "Or picking up bottles along the road," I said.

I was miles from the truth.

"Maybe so. But it weren't no fine day for Frank, never was. His granddaddy didn't leave him squat by way of money. He spent his days at the fillin' station, livin' outta that old trailer out back. That inner-state bypass killed the traffic, an' took what was left a that bidnuss with it. He didn't make much more 'n nuthin'. Guess that's why he had Justus."

"Justus was his meal ticket."

"Frank told me once he liked to pepper the dog's food with gunpowder. Said it put fire in his belly. I reckon he was right. All the same, Justus was special to Frank. Like dogs are prone to doin' Justus was all about Frank. Well, I guess so long as Frank fed him."

"The dog loved him."

"I don't know 'bout that. Dog didn't know no better than what he had, that's all. I don't believe Frank fed him too good, but he fed him just 'nuff. On the day, was purty clear Frank had been doin' him some serious drinkin'. Sorta picture come outta the mess he left behind. Frank never gave much thought to cleanin' his guns when he was sober, givin' how he mostly never was. He musta forgot the shotgun was loaded. Bam, he was dead as a doorknob."

"Did people think it was suicide?"

"Folks gonna believe what they wanna believe. It weren't no suicide, he shot hiself in the armpit, so you know it were accidental. Shotgun musta spooked that dog somethin' fierce. Justus used the gifts God gave him and tore out that front door an' he 'as off in the wind, free as a bird. Thus endeth the life a Frank James Wilson. I'd say I miss him. I wonder sometimes what woulda happened if his momma weren't so damn nuts."

"It's a sad story, but I'm not sure…"

"That ain't the end of the story."

"Oh?"

"It's why you need to listen 'stead of talkin'. You see, right about time Frank's life was drainin' out, Mister Peter Gentry was parkin' his truck on side the road, fixin' to do him some bottle huntin'. He parked at marker ten, like always, and got goin'. He liked that stretch, said it was near lined with money. He'd got to marker twelve, crossed the road and headed on back to his truck, pickin' up the goods as he went."

"How old was mister Gentry at the time?"

"How the hell should I know? Old enough to be retired and pickin' up bottles aside the road."

"I can look it up…"

"You do that. Now Gentry, I 'spose he was lookin' down at the ground searchin' for booty, and that's why he didn't take no notice of the dog 'til he was about on top of him. I'll betchya good money he's right surprised to come up on Justus gnawin' on that chunk'a roadkill. Mule dear, few days dead."

"The dog was eating a deer?"

"Part of one anyway."

"And you know this…"

"I seen it, but you're gettin' out in front again."

"I'll save my questions for…"

"I bet you will. Now Gentry, he probably done raised up

that stick and made all kinda ruckus at that dog. But a eatin' dog ain't in no mood to be disturbed. Justus lit into that old man an' weren't nobody 'round to stop him. Coroner told me it didn't take the old man long to die, but I wonder. Justus musta found Gentry to his likin' 'cuz he give up on that road kill an' set to feastin' on the old man instead. Them folks what drove up on it near went right by. Thought it was just another part of that deer. Then they got themselves a up-close look. Giant-ass dog covered in blood and guts, it weren't no sight for the tender hearted."

"They didn't stop, who can blame 'em? I wouldn't a stopped neither. They come in my store hot 'n bothered, one of 'em outside throwin' up all over the place. I rung up the Sheriff, him and me rode down to see what's what. It were a damn ugly mess, I tell you what. Sheriff tried to shoot Justus and dang if that dog didn't take off like a rocket, headin' west. Don't see how he moved so fast with a belly full of Gentry, but he sure 'nuff did."

"Was the dog shot? Did he kill the dog?"

"Hell if I know. Sheriff, he laughed an' radio'd for someone to come fetch what was left a Gentry. Weren't never no love lost between Sheriff and them Gentrys. As for what got et and what got not et, I ain't gonna tell ya. I ain't never gonna forget it, y'all know that. Me and Sheriff decided ain't nobody need to know. Coroner wrote it up a heart attack 'n when folks wonder'd why that casket was closed, we didn't say nuthin' 'bout nuthin'."

"How many people know the truth?"

"You don't believe me?"

"Of course I believe you, it's…"

"Me, Sheriff, one or two folks I may have let slip…"

"Like Miss Annie?"

"Includin' Annie."

"And the dog?"

"Ain't nobody had reason to go lookin' for that dog. I didn't want that beast livin' in my yard. Ain't no chain strong 'nuff for me to trust Justus. I don't wanna know where he went. Hightailin' away from me was good enough for me."

"Frank's kin from up Apalachee stuck him in the ground betwixt his mamma and granddaddy. They ain't had money for a stone, so I made sure he had a little somethin' with his name on it stuck over top his grave. Least I could do, I 'spose."

He fell silent again. This time a tear escaped his eye and ran down his cheek.

"Mister Gentry..."

"What 'as left a Gentry got stuck in the family plot, big ol' polished-up stone over top. Reads 'Happy They Who Fearin' God Fear Nothin' Else.' I think it's a lot of horse shit but that's just me."

"I feel like there's more to this story Mister Barnsley."

"That thar's the story I got, you ain't gonna git it nowhere else."

"What about Frank's father?"

"His daddy? Round here, some thangs is best let alone, if you catch my meanin'."

We sat listening to a clock ticking, then the old man rubbed his chin and said, "I reckon you'll be wantin' to git on outta here. Git some of that saltwater taffy, come all the way from Savannah. Drop some at Annie's, probably why she sent you here, just to git herself some candy. You ain't gotta pay. Them sodas in the case is ice cold, practically froze, good on a day like this, quarter apiece if you want 'em. Don't you toss 'em empties out ya window. Ain't no old man out pickin' 'em up now days and they ain't worth a nickel no more."

"Thank you, much appreciated. Mister Barnsley, do you think they'd have any records, anything related to this story, here in town, maybe at the police station? Or the library?"

Anything…"

"You don't believe me, do ya?"

"I most certainly believe you, yes sir. I wonder what the official line is on these events, how the local authorities or historians recorded it."

"The 'local authorities…' they recorded it by shuttin' up about it. That's how it works 'round here. Ain't no records, but you go on over to the station, I ain't got no problem with it. Down Main, hang a left at Third, the station gonna be right thar in front a ya. Now, you don't mind, I got me some work to see to…"

"May I take your picture. Maybe a few shots of the store too?"

"I reckon I'm dressed for it, ain't I?"

"Yes sir, be right back."

I carried the recorder out to my truck and grabbed my camera. Photos weren't a part of my project, but I'd started taking them to help bind the stories to the people, and the places. Plus, everyone knows what a picture is worth. I didn't want to miss out on that value.

When I went back inside, Mister Barnsley sat up straight and looked at me. He grimaced and scowled, either from discomfort, or disdain, or both.

I knelt in an aisle and snapped two shots, then lowered the camera. As soon as he relaxed I took two more, one of which caught him looking up at the Bible verses painted on the brick wall. I replaced the lens cap and grabbed two bags of candy for Miss Annie and two sodas for me, so cold they hurt my hand. I dropped two dollars on the counter. "Thank you again Mister Barnsley, your time is much appreciated. Your story too. I'll come back and see you again if I have more questions."

"You do that," he said, "now git, I got work to do."

"Yes sir, goodbye Mister Barnsley."

"Go on, git," I heard him say as the screen door slammed shut behind me.

I took a few shots of the building and its surroundings, a picket fence around a dirt yard under an ancient oak tree. On the other side a derelict barn, so rough it looked like it could fall in at any moment. I opened the door to my truck, set the candy and one soda inside, then opened the second soda on the latch of my door. I took an icy slurp, then climbed in behind the wheel.

I parked in the shade of a three story building across the street from the police station. Then I wasted half an hour trying to find any record of the death of Peter Gentry. There was nothing, the clerk assured me, beyond the coroner's report that the old man had died of a heart attack while riding his bicycle along the road now named after him. The officer was polite but sent me on my way with, "Young man, I appreciate your persistence, but you need to understand some folks around Morganville liked to tell tales, and those same folks often have a loose relationship with the truth." He didn't say which folks were which, and I decided not to open that can of worms.

It was 4:00 PM when I pulled up to Esther's. The restaurant wasn't busy yet, just two customers at a corner table. Miss Annie smiled at me from behind the counter and motioned at a stool in front of her. I sat down and presented the two bags of saltwater taffy.

"Gift from Mister Barnsley."

She laughed, shaking her head, "That old coot knows I hate this stuff." She walked to her register, filled a bowl with one bag, then tossed the other onto a shelf below. Back around the counter, she smiled again. "Are you buyin' your own supper today?"

"Yes ma'am," I said, "Quite the story, as promised. Not sure it's right for the project, we'll have to wait and see."

"What do you mean, not right? A rich old man gets eaten alive by the dog of the man he wronged decades earlier. That's a story. Heck, Thomas, that's a movie in the makin'."

I grinned back at her smile. "An after school special maybe, but I need more information, something to corroborate Barnsley's story. It's a good story, for sure, but there's gotta be more to it. And so many questions..."

"What else do you need to know?"

"For starters, who was Frank Wilson's father? You can't leave that mystery unsolved. And Mister Barnsley said the sheriff laughed when he saw what happened to Mister Gentry. Why would he laugh? Why did they fake the coroner's report? That one worries me, the official record doesn't support the story..."

"Hold on, slow it down," she said. She placed a tumbler of tea and a bowl of pickle chips in front of me. She walked through the kitchen into a small office. I heard the metal scrape of a file cabinet drawer, followed by the drawer slamming shut. She re-emerged with an inches-thick aged-yellow manila folder in her hand and plunked it down on the counter with a thud. "Go on, open it."

I raised an eyebrow and she nodded her head. I pealed the folder open and the first thing I saw nearly nocked me off my stool.

It was a black and white photograph, taken in front of Esther's, from a time when the surrounding buildings were well kept. A car from a bygone era parked in front of Esther's, it appeared to be new in the photograph. Leaning against the car was a handsome teenage boy, but he could have been a young man, it was hard to say given his size, and suit and tie. He held a bowler hat in his hand.

He looked shockingly similar to Annie's son, my friend, Lewis. Lewis and I spent a lot of time together. Camping, fishing, studying, drinking, you name it. We were roommates, and about as close as two college boys could be, without it being a romantic relationship. His skin wasn't particularly dark, but it was evident that my best friend had a mixed heritage. And here in this folder was a photo that could have been Lewis, if Lewis had lived decades earlier.

I was speechless long enough for Miss Annie to get impatient, "What's wrong Thomas, cat gotchya tongue?"

"Yes, as a matter of fact…is that…"

"Frank Wilson, the one and same."

"He looks a lot like…."

"He does."

"I don't understand. How old is he in this picture?"

"Fourteen, his first day of high school. Frankie might not have meant much to the people down in Morganville, but up here in Apalachee, he was kin, and we loved him from his first day to his last, just like his momma, my grandmother's sister, my grand-aunt."

"Why didn't you tell me before…"

"Before you heard the old man's sad sack story? Because sometimes it's better to hear the worst part of the story first, wouldn't you agree?"

"Yes ma'am, I would. But what about…"

"It's all in there, everything you need to know. Take your time, read on through it, I've got customers to look after. You want cornbread or white bread with your supper?"

"You know I gotta have that cornbread Miss Annie."

"That's what I thought. You be careful not to spill anything. I don't want to see your fingerprints on any of that paper either."

"Yes ma'am, I'll be careful."

And I was, even as glass after glass of tea appeared in front of me and the biggest-ever platter of chicken, green beans, black-eyed peas, macaroni casserole, and collard greens with ham landed on the counter. It was twice the size of a normal meal. I took it to mean she meant what she said when she told me take my time. I also took it to mean I would not be leaving with the folder.

It seemed Miss Annie had appointed herself the local historian, and her folder of photos, news clipping, church announcements and letters, all together represented a sort of library of congress for her family and the broader Apalachee community. I became so engrossed, I didn't notice the passage of time, as the restaurant filled and emptied and filled again, then emptied once more. Miss Annie flipped the sign on the door to 'Closed' and said good night to her last customer, and her lone employee. I heard her pull down the roller shades, closing us in together, blocking out the rest of the world.

It was approaching 10:00 PM. She cleared her register, cleaned up around me, then poured herself a cup of coffee. She sat down at one of the larger tables. "Thomas, come on over here with that, let's hear what you learned so far."

"Yes ma'am," I said. I'd had so much caffeine and sugar my head was buzzing and my hands were shaking. I nearly spilled the folder but managed to keep it all together, and mostly in order. I placed it on the table and helped myself to a glass of water, then sat down across from her.

"What do you think? You got yourself a story now?"

"I believe I do," I said. "How do you think people are gonna feel about all this?"

"What people?" she said, raising her hands and looking around. "My people? You think people in Apalachee are gonna care about a truth they've lived with all their lives? A truth that paints a better picture of them, and their… relations?"

"I guess I was thinking about the people in Morganville. Seems like they've got a lot of secrets they've been keeping all these years."

"And that, young Thomas, is why it's a story. Go ahead, tell me what you learned tonight."

"Well, the headline, if there's only one, is Frank's father. I had my suspicions, the way he teared up when he talked about Frank…."

"Jimmy Barnsley shed a tear over my cousin Frankie? I never thought I'd see the day."

"Wouldn't Frank be your…"

"A cousin is a cousin, and a cousin is kin. We don't care how many first or seconds or times removed."

"Understood. He shed a few tears over Suzy too."

"That doesn't surprise me, I heard he cried a river at her funeral. Didn't see it myself. I'll give him that, he did love her. Not enough to marry her though."

"Seems like he wasn't the only man in Morganville who had a female friend in Apalachee."

"And the road ran both ways. Still does. That surprise you?"

"Yes, but if I understand the history, that sort of thing goes all the way back to…"

"To when such relations weren't necessarily consensual."

"That's how I read it. If Barnsley is Frank's father, where'd the name Wilson come from? And what's with the stories about your grandfather? Barnsley said…"

"They picked Wilson because there weren't any Wilsons in Morganville at the time. Did he say my grandfather was a drunk and a womanizer and a thief?"

"Barnsley said Frank's grandfather spent Frank's inheritance on booze and women."

"I imagine he did say that. I'm sad to say, he would be partly correct. His grandfather took Frank in, but he was not a perfect man. In fact Frank's grandmother kicked her husband out of the house, but they stayed married. But he took the money Suzy left behind and paid off all her debts, made sure her property would never be a burden to Frank. Put the rest in the bank and set it up so Frank would have it when he turned eighteen. But every now and then, he dipped into that well and had himself a big time in Atlanta or Savanah, or wherever he wanted to land for a weekend. Always said he would pay it back but never did. Not until he died and left Frankie some acreage he owned along the river. But yes, I suppose there's some truth in what the old man told you."

"Then why was Frank poor?"

"He was never poor, Thomas, he just didn't spend money on himself. There's a big difference. You know my church, the one I can never get my son to attend because he's always off galavanting around with you?"

"I'm afraid to answer that question."

"You should be. My church, the first brick-built church in Apalachee. Frankie, my cousin, paid for it to be built. He was never poor. My family has never been poor."

"Then why…"

"Because that's how some folks like to see us out here in Apalachee, nothing more than that. Did Jimmy tell you he's the one who found Frankie?"

"He didn't mention that. If he was first on the scene, how was he back at his store when Justus killed Mister Gentry?"

She smiled, but it wasn't a happy look.

"I guess he didn't tell you they died two days apart."

"He said they died the same day. Did he set the dog loose? He said he was afraid of Justus."

"Maybe he was, maybe he wasn't. He's the one that gave that dog to Frankie. Got him from a breeder someplace outside of Columbus. Helped train him too. He went to pay Frankie a visit, found him lying dead in his kitchen. The dog had taken a few bites out of Frankie's face."

"Oh God…"

"It's been known to happen," she said, then tapped the folder, "you can read about it. There's an article in here, bottom of the stack."

"Frank let the dog run off after it…"

"No. He told me he took the dog the next day and set him loose along Route 12, somewhere near mile marker ten, where the road curves toward the river. Said he left some food out there for the dog to eat, so it wouldn't follow him home. There was nothing out there back then, but it was the main road between Apalachee and Morganville. Are you starting to see the picture?"

I didn't know what to say, so I kept quiet. My mind was bouncing off one idea, one fact, one story after another. Miss Annie drained her coffee, set the mug down, and folded her hands on the table.

"Why did he lie to me? What's the point?"

She looked me in the eyes, like she was reading my thoughts. "I know your people aren't from the South, so it may take you some time to connect all the dots. Here's what I want you to do." She laid one hand on the folder like she was swearing an oath on a Bible. "You take this, I'm gonna trust you with my history. You make copies, I know they have a Xerox machine at the library in Athens. Then you send the originals back with Lewis, this Sunday," she said, emphasizing 'Sunday.' "I want to see my son and listen to his angelic voice singing God's praise for the first time in a year of Sundays. Can you do that?"

I knew I could make copies at the library. Not certain I could get Lewis to go to church with his mother. But 'no' didn't feel like an option.

"Yes ma'am, I can do that."

"Good, now go on home. You shouldn't be driving that rattle-trap truck of yours this late. Next time you come this way, think about having my son drive you. His car has air conditioning and you look about as wilted as a bad head of lettuce."

"Yes ma'am," I said and pulled out my wallet to settle my bill.

"No, you keep your money, supper's on me. You only got part of the story down in Morganville, and you've got some work to do for me, don't you?"

I put my wallet away and smiled, "That I do Miss Annie, thank you."

"Alright then, mosey on. You tell my son his Momma loves him and misses him and she looks forward to seeing him in church this Sunday. You're welcome to come along too, if you like."

"Will do, Miss Annie. Goodnight. Thank you again. This was not the day I was expecting."

"It seldom is. Goodnight Thomas, drive careful."

I stepped into the night, and she closed and locked the door behind me. I looked up at the shimmering stars and wondered if there were other places in the world like Apalachee, other people like Lewis and Annie, James and Frank and Suzy.

I knew there were plenty of places like Morganville, I'd seen more than a few. As I pondered the implications, I wondered how many of those places had satellite towns, then considered Morganville might be the satellite and Apalachee the planet.

A car roared through the intersection, dust swirling in clouds behind it, glittering in the yellow glow of the lone streetlight. It reminded me of the late hour. I got in my truck, rolled down the window and fired up the engine. I placed the folder on the seat and put my camera bag on top to keep everything in place. I turned on the radio and headed north towards home.

I was in no hurry. I had an entire world to ponder, a

multitude of dots to connect, stars of an inner sky. Some had already formed into constellations, others were still scattered, their connections still obscure. I drove on through the darkness, bright moonlight flashing through the pines.

I came to the conclusion that no matter how well we get to know each other, we will all have some mystery about us, some stories we don't tell, some past we don't share. I didn't know why Miss Annie had shared her's with me, and I hadn't thought to ask. But I resolved to honor her story, her family's history. Not just James Barnsley's version of it, but all of it, his and hers, and theirs alike.

I rolled to a stop sign in the center of Watkinsville, the well-lit streets empty except for me. I saw a small dog sitting by the curb in front of a drug store. I pulled into a parking space near the dog, got out, and knelt down on the sidewalk. I whistled softly. The dog stared at me and didn't move. I sat down cross-legged and whistled again, and the dog stood and walked toward me.

He came close and sniffed my outstretched hand. He let me pet his head and scratch behind his ears. He was young, a couple of months at most. His paws were huge for his size. He had a smooth brindle coat, filthy with caked-on dirt, fleas crawling all over him. His belly was bloated, a sign he had worms. If he was anyone's dog, they didn't deserve him.

He surprised me by crawling into my lap, and stared up at me with eyes that could melt a glacier. I stroked his back and he started shaking, then rewarded my kindness by urinating on my leg. I laughed and scooped him up, put him on the floorboard on the passenger side of the truck and got back on the road. He stayed where I put him, and by the time I pulled up to my house he was fast asleep.

I'll never know why he became a part of this story, but he did, by fate or my good fortune.

Upon seeing him Lewis said, "Where did you get this ugly

dog?"

"He's not ugly," I replied, "he's handsome, and I already love him. You wait and see, he's gonna grow up and be something special, I guarantee it."

"Fine, he's a prince, but the prince has fleas, get him out of the house, dogs belong in the yard."

"No way, he stays with me. Fleas are easy, a bath, then a little lemon juice and warm water, he'll be all set."

Lewis smiled his mother's smile and shook his head in disbelief, "Man, you're crazy," he said. He turned and walked toward the kitchen, "What's the mix on the flea-killer cocktail?"

"Fifty-fifty," I said, "use the bottled juice." I carried the dog into the bathroom and set him down in the tub. He shook again when I turned on the water. When it was warm, I cupped my hands and slowly soaked him. The water ran off dark grey from the filth, spotted with fleas floating down the drain. Lewis entered with a bowl of liquid and set it on the toilet.

"One flea killer, ready when you are. You should dump some on yourself too."

"Very funny. By the way, your mother is expecting you for church on Sunday, I told her I'd make sure you showed up."

"Then you're coming with me."

"As long as I don't have to sing."

"You've got a fine voice, you're too chickenshit to use it outside the shower is all. Church might do you some good."

"Says the kettle to the pot."

I scrubbed the dog with my own shampoo, then rinsed him and started pouring the lemon juice blend over him. More fleas evacuated and were washed away. I kept going until I thought I had them all, then rinsed the dog again. Lewis stayed to watch the entire process. When I finished, he handed me a clean towel.

"Okay," he said, "not so ugly after all. Maybe a little on the handsome side. You got a name for him?"

"Yes," I said, "I'm gonna call him Justice."

Lewis laughed, "Why are you gonna name the dog Justice?"

"Because," I said, "I don't think there's enough of it in the world. Gotta start someplace. Might as well start with him."

The Emerson Incident

Life on the generation ship ESS *SeienSiefreundlichRücklauf* was generally uneventful as it cruised through space on its way to star system Wolf 1069. Wolfy for short. There was the occasional rise of a cult, an opportunistic mutiny or two, and the equally opportunistic civil war now and again, but none of these had as lasting an impact as the "Emerson Incident."

The mega-space-wheel turned ceaselessly, decade after decade, centrifugal force creating a 1-G environment for generations of humans making the slow crawl across interstellar space at a leisurely 283,490.52 miles per hour.

The ship was fully automated. No one had a thing to do but eat, sleep, drink, and produce the next generation of passengers. Most people had gotten quite good at these activities, especially the last one.

In anticipation of the monotony of the journey, the builders of the ship established a school, named after a well-liked employee, drawn by lottery, of the ship's builder. The Emerson School of Culture, Art, and Performative Excellence, aka the ESCAPE, would train a select group from each generation in the entertainment arts.

These young people, the best each generation had to offer, spent their lives learning how to sing, dance, play instruments, and write amazing books, all to amuse those passengers who would otherwise go insane watching the distant stars drift languidly by their portals.

One day, the newly elected Captain of the *SeienSiefreundlichRücklauf* made a decision that would reverberate across history. He decided, mostly out of boredom, to stop the big wheel from spinning, to shake things up a bit. He thought it best to keep it a secret, a Grand

Surprise. After centuries of ceaseless turning, the Big Spin was about to become the Big Stop.

It was, of course, a disaster. But in an odd sort of way, a way only possible in space, the Big Stop changed everything for the better.

While the Big Stop was felt all over the ship, its most profound impact was felt in the cafeteria of the ESCAPE, a magical place filled with off-key vocals, off-beat drummers, Zero-G dancers, and volumes of bad poetry. Students of the ESCAPE were the best of the rest, and they knew it. Nothing held them back when the spirit moved them to perform, not even a dearth of talent. They were kids, they were noisy, some of them had skills, and it was lunchtime.

They spent a lot of time watching themselves in the giant mirrors that lined the walls of the cafeteria.

Gertrude Snicklefritz, the finest mediocre ballerina in the ship's company, loved to Glisser and Sauter her way through the cafeteria, holding her tray high in the air, its arugula salad with synth-oil and vinegar dressing, spinning and swooping over the heads of her fellow students. Her daily court convened along the inner wall of the dining hall, a location that afforded her the maximum dance floor between food and table.

Tommy Dank, the ship's finest clown, couldn't stand Gertrude Snicklefritz. Every time she Elanced by his seat, he felt a powerful urge to trip her. He never did, despite the size of his shoes. He wasn't an evil clown, he just didn't like Gertrude. On the day of the Big Stop, a few drops of dressing spilled off her plate and stained his clown suit.

Furious, Tommy Dank had had enough. He knew he'd never get that oil out of his chartreuse lapel. He wanted revenge, and he knew how to get it. He waited until Gertrude took her seat, to the applause of her retinue, then he struck.

Pulling a clown spoon from his clown pocket, he scooped

up a thick glob of kimchi and took aim. He pulled back the spoon and let loose his catapult of spiced cabbage with the expertise of a Frenchman with a trebuchet. Off the ordnance went, and his aim was dead-on perfect.

Gertrude never saw it coming.

A young lady seated at the far end of the table did see it coming, but as she was the least of the BFFs, she said nothing.

The weaponized kimchi landed against the young Ms. Snicklefritz's face with a resounding squishy splat.

The entire room, for once, fell silent.

Gertrude scanned the room, her eyes narrow, face red, seeking the source of the delicious but odiferous kimchi. Her stare landed on Tommy Dank, smiling back at her, holding up his giant clown spoon, ruby-red lips grinning ear to ear.

Tommy pointed at the stains on his lapel and shouted, "You get what you give."

Tommy, in his naiveté, or perhaps ignorance, failed to realize there is no more dangerous creature in the universe than an angry ballerina.

Gertrude surveyed her retinue and asked with a growl, "Who's with me?"

When Tommy saw the table of menacing ballerinas Tourne as one, he knew the battle was joined. He had his Clown Alley close at hand, they were always up for a brawl, though theirs usually involved rubber chickens and pails of confetti, not their lunch.

The space between them cleared like an old western movie, just as a student from the film club let out his best Spaghetti Western Whistle. Sergio Leone had no greater fan.

Unlike normal people, Gertrude Snicklefritz wasn't afraid of clowns. Not even an entire army of them would deter her vengeance. She scraped the now-cool glob of kimchi from her face, formed it into a ball, and prepared to let loose her entire ballerina might at Tommy Dank's face. Gertrude pulled back her arm, then flung the kimchi-ball forward as hard as she could.

It was that very moment, with all her momentum going forward, the Great Wheel of the *SeienSiefreundlichRücklauf* stopped spinning, and the 1-G gravity that held them all to the deck was gone.

Gertrude went down, thudding her head against the deck before bouncing back up and spinning away toward the aforementioned mirrors. When she saw her reflection, she was so taken by her own beauty and grace, spinning weightless and free, she forgot to brace herself as she approached the wall. A second thud, and she ricocheted right out of the room.

Meanwhile, the kimchi missile she'd launched missed Tommy Dank and found its way into the face of one Mary Jane Sessions. Mary Jane had no target for her wrath, but that didn't stop her. She braced herself, then grabbed the nearest chaco-taco, an especially rare confection, and sent it hurling through the weightlessness.

Mary Jane could see that all-out war was at hand. She began to gather more weapons from trays and bowls and plates, even as the other members of her Ska band formed a protective circle around her.

The chaco-taco, in all its gooey melting glory, made a beeline for Scarlett I'dareya's updo, and before you could say "You Better Work," the kids from the vaunted Runway School had joined the fight. As Scarlett let loose a barrage of meatballs, her sisters-in-arms formed a daisy-chain barricade, reinforced by layered loops of duct tape. They tucked in, and stood as one.

The other kids in the room, those who had yet to be struck by any flying foodstuff, shouted 'YOLO' as more food began to fly in all directions, for no reason other than it could. Such a terrible waste, and they knew it. They also knew every bit of organic material would be recycled. They'd be eating their mess again soon enough.

Unfortunately, most of the ESCAPE kids didn't understand gravity, or more precisely, the lack thereof. Before long, bodies were flying about the room in a furious gyrating flurry, as kids who threw mashed potatoes suddenly found themselves getting smacked in the face by the same said projectile. Some, the smart ones, held onto a table or bench, and as their ammo ran low they reached up and grabbed whatever was passing overhead.

Tacos, grilled cheese sandwiches, fried fish, anything they could grab, they flung back into the maelstrom. For those not slamming into the mirrored walls, which acted as force multipliers for the chaos, it was a glorious time.

The young writers, for their part, stayed clear of the melee in order to document it for history's sake. One poet recited feverish lines and wrote them as she went, an extemporaneous masterpiece that would one day be required learning for aspiring poets. Both the rappers and the rockers gave her props.

It was one such writer, Ladiv Erog, who first realized they were witnessing more than a food fight in space (which, admittedly, was a historical first). They were witnessing the birth of a revolution.

A student of historical fiction, she recorded nothing, preferring instead to watch, and experience, and store away the facts for later. Once the event was over, she would use her memory to shape whatever narrative she felt appropriate and most engaging, while still following the basic outline of the truth, if she could.

But the battle lasted too long for her. She had plans later that day, and besides, it was getting boring. After a time, she couldn't take it anymore.

"Enough!" she cried, drawing on the one drama class she'd

ever taken, "enough of all this, all of you. This is not who we are. We are not heathens. We are not animals. We are not wasters of food. We are artists, all of us. Stop this madness. Lend me your ears and I will tell you of your true enemy."

Ladiv's timing was perfect. No sooner had her words left her lips than the enormous wheel of the generation ship began to spin again. Gravity returned, and with it, sanity. All that was floating and adrift in the room dropped to the floor with a cacophony of disgusting sounds.

"Tell us," a banjo player shouted, "tell us what you know. How did this happen? Who are we to blame?"

"This is your parents' fault," she shouted back, *"They* elected a fool to be Captain. Only he can cause the wheel to stop. This is his doing. Join me, to the bridge we must go. Bring what you can, a cheese stick, a chicken strip, a spoon, a fork, a spork if you must, whatever you can carry. To the bridge my friends. Let's go. Let's take back our ship!"

So it was that history was made. The once genteel students of the ESCAPE formed an army and stormed the bridge of the *SeienSiefreundlichRücklauf.* Soon they controlled the ship, or at least the part of it that symbolized control of the ship. They made a show of hands and voted out the Captain, thus ending the Tenancy of the Weird And Terrible, as it became known. Their uprising ushered in a new era of peace, stability, and everlasting gravitational living.

These young people, Generation-G as they became known, also forever changed the way the people chose their leaders.

From that day forward, every man, woman and child (over the age of sixteen - they didn't go nuts) was required to vote, unless they didn't feel like it, or had a written excuse from their doctor, or their lawyer, or a really close friend who knew they shouldn't have a hand in decision making.

As for the instigators of the battle, Tommy, upon seeing Gertrude's unconscious body drift out of the cafeteria, became overwhelmed with guilt. Since a sad clown is a cliche clown, as soon as gravity returned Tommy rushed to Gertrude's side.

When Gertrude awoke in Tommy's arms, seeing his sad clown frown turn into tears of joy, Gertrude knew why she never feared clowns. It was because she'd always loved Tommy Dank.

Tommy, seeing a smile on Gertrude's face upon her awakening, with a special sparkle in her eyes, realized he never hated Gertrude Snicklefritz. He simply wanted more of her, but didn't know how to get her.

So it was that Tommy Dank and Gertrude Snicklefritz put aside their differences, fell in love, took up Dagga farming in the zero-G tube at the center of the ship, and made lots of happily mediocre babies.

The Snicklefritz-Dank union set a shining example for others to follow. They proved that even the most different of people, a somewhat skilled angry ballerina and a frustrated clown with a drip on his shoulder, could form a loving union and grow sweet delights in space, with or without gravity.

Their Bake Sales were legendary, their crops became the new currency, their lives became a religion, and their descendants became its High Priests and Priestesses. The Faithful maintained the Word across the lightyears.

Theirs was a cult the people could live with. The Dankists eventually took over the ship in the most mellow of elections. Their first order of business was to rename their vessel the *Pakalolo*. Easier to say and spell, they reasoned.

At long last the ship arrived at Wolfy. The passengers were safe, sound, and perfectly mellow. On the auspicious day, when the mighty spinning wheel of the *Pakalolo* arrived at humanity's new home in the Cosmos, the Captain called for a day of celebration. It wasn't much different from any other day onboard the ship, but she made a speech and some special brownies, both of which were well received.

But the Captain was wise and decided to scout the planet before using precious fuel to stop the Big Wheel and enter orbit around their destination. A group of intrepid explorers went down to the surface of the planet. They planted a flag and some Dagga seeds, dubbed their new world Chillsville, then marveled at their own awesomeness.

After a pause to watch the wind blow, as the Big Wheel neared the point of no return, passing right through the heart of the system, the explorers returned to their shuttle, ready to spread the news of the new world.

Heady Snicklefritz-Dank slipped into the pilot's seat, looked around at his companions, and said the words that would forever change the course of human history.

"Okay, which one of you knuckleheads has the keys?"

Cloudland

My Uncle Joseph held a special place in my life. For my seventeenth birthday I received a postcard, an image of Carnival, drag queens and near-naked men parading down Commercial Street in Provincetown. It was his way of letting me know I had an ally, should I ever need one.

The cancer was aggressive. He was diagnosed in September, and dead by February. Like many single men of his generation, he didn't care much for doctors, until they couldn't be avoided. The poor timing of his death required me to make the five hour drive from Boston, Massachusetts to Hudson, New York, in the dead of winter for the reading of his will. His lawyer, Sandy, insisted on the location, making vague reference to binding stipulations I'd be required to accommodate if I wanted the full inheritance.

My uncle's estate was in the mountains of Northeastern Pennsylvania, overlooking the Delaware River. He'd left me his property, and an enormous sum of money. The compound included several buildings and an extensive art collection. I never knew how wealthy my uncle was, and had never visited his estate. Not for a lack of interest, but for a lack of an invitation. When Sandy called me to discuss my inheritance, I found it strange to go to bed a struggling writer, and wake up a wealthy man.

Upon arriving in Hudson, I learned the will contained two significant stipulations.

First, I had to spend one month in the house within one week of the reading. This was, in fact, convenient for me. I was going through a breakup. The trip would be a welcome escape, and the time away would give me an opportunity to plan my next move.

The more problematic stipulation required me to keep the property. I could not sell it, nor could I rent it. Thankfully, there was no debt against it, and ample funds had been provided for its maintenance. It was mine for life, like it or not, but I could not monetize it as I had originally hoped.

"What if I hate it?" I asked.

"You're gonna love it," Sandy insisted. "Fifty gorgeous acres, from the mountaintop to the river. But be careful, the road up the mountain get's a little twisty, there could be snow. You have a four wheel drive, a truck, something like that?"

"I'll manage. How long is the drive to…why is it called Cloudland?"

"The altitude, of course. It's the highest point in the entire range. No one around for miles, except Brendan. Brendan was my first client here, seems like forever ago. He sold the land to your uncle, gave him quite the deal. He lives in a castle, can you believe it? A castle, a mere hop, skip, and jump to the west of your place. He's quite charming. You can see it, the castle, part of it, from the swimming pool. He and your uncle were very close."

"Sounds like a fairly tale. How long?"

"Oh, I'd say, three hours, if you don't make too many stops."

"Why would I stop?"

"Food, alcohol, gasoline, sightseeing, who knows? You should load up on provisions here in Hudson. Narrowsburg shuts down with the sun. It's a fine little town, very gay on summer weekends. There's…"

"Are we finished?"

"Yes, unless you'd like to join me for dinner…"

"I won't be staying in Hudson."

He placed the documents and keys into a box and my journey began. I took his advice, and made a few stops on my way out of Hudson to load up on supplies. It was late in the day by the time I got underway.

A few hours later I crossed the river into Pennsylvania. The darkness and the winding road made for slow going. When I turned onto the private road up to the property, the full moon was layering the valley in shades of blue and gray. I entered a clearing that stretched beyond my field of vision and came to a white one story building, the guest house, a converted stable.

A stand of trees cast moon shadows across my path. I briefly considered exploring the guest house, until I saw two green eyes glowing at me from the periphery of my headlights. I took it as a sign to keep moving.

The main house was a study in rectilinear modernism, clad in horizontal sheets of steel, trimmed in white. Overgrown junipers fought each other for space along the facade. Small rectangular windows were placed low, larger windows lined the upper section. The pool was a short distance uphill from the house, and was itself overlooked by an equally severe structure. Lights led to a parking pad between the house and garage. I parked and entered the house, surprised to find it unlocked.

The main floor was open space, with a galley kitchen behind one wall. A grand piano held court opposite the fireplace. A small lamp cast shadows throughout. I started to go back to my vehicle to get my supplies, when a commanding voice called out to me, bringing me to a sudden stop.

"Welcome home, Christopher."

I spun around to see a man on the sofa in front of the fireplace, propped up on one elbow, a leather coat slung over the padded arm behind his head.

"Who the hell are you?"

"I'm Brendan, your neighbor. I'm sorry, I didn't intend to

frighten you. Sandy asked me to prepare the house. I thought I'd wait for you and give you a tour, help you settle in. I was expecting you much earlier."

"Sorry to disappoint, it's been a long day…"

"Not at all. But I've upset you, what a terrible first impression I'm making, I'm so sorry. I'll leave, we can speak in the morning, I'm sure you can do with some rest."

Though he had startled me, I found my self wishing he would stay. There was something about his voice, the tone, his unplaceable accent, his never-ending smile. He looked about my age, a bit shorter, muscular but not thick. He came toward me, thighs flexing under tight-fitting jeans, chest pushing out from under his flannel shirt, sleeves rolled up, a meaty pair of forearms on display. Porcelain skin, green eyes, red hair, a day's growth across his square jaw, bisected by a dimpled chin. It would be an understatement to say my attraction to him was instant, and powerful.

"You surprised me, that's all, you don't have to rush off. I could use a little help unloading my supplies."

"It would be my pleasure."

The house was built into the slope of the land, living area above, bedrooms below. We stocked the kitchen, then Brendan led me to the lower lever.

"There are three bedrooms, linens are freshly laundered, the primary suite has the best view."

"You went to a lot of trouble," I said, "How well did you know my uncle?"

"It was no trouble for me, your uncle's housekeeper did the work, I slept on the job. Your uncle and I were the best of friends. Joey was a gentleman, a wonderful neighbor, truly the best. I miss him terribly, his life was all too brief. I hope his passing was gentle. Were you with him?"

"Yes," I said, "but he was long gone before his body died."

"He loved you, you know, in his way. Talked about you all

the time. He was quite proud of your work."

"I know he loved me. As for the work, well, he was always a generous man."

Moonlight flowing in through a glass wall filled the room. It overlooked a field gently sloping toward a low wall in the distance. Brendan looked out at the terrain, his gaze following something moving across the field. I looked out, but saw nothing.

He placed his hand on my back, between my shoulders. The effect was immediate. Waves of excitement pulsed through my body. Stomach tightened, legs trembled, pulse quickened. My body had never had such a reaction to a man's touch. It was unlike me to allow it, but I found myself welcoming this strange and unexpected intimacy — without hesitation. He slid his hand upward, and took gentle hold of my neck. My body was prepared to surrender to whatever he wanted, to submit to his will even as my mind tried, and failed, to quash my desire. He splayed his fingers and clasped the base of my skull. He turned my head away from his, angled my eyes down, and pointed with his free hand. I desperately wanted to control the shaking in my legs, to slow my breathing, to push back against arousal. I was losing on all fronts.

"There," he whispered, his voice caressing my ear, "along the tree-line, beyond the deadfall, do you see her?"

The glowing eyes of the beast floated in the shadows. It stepped into the open and stared at us. A monstrous wolf, shoulders higher than my waist, shimmering mane cascading down its broad chest. Such a magnificent terror, standing calmly in the night.

"Her name is Orla," he said, moving his hand to the small of my back, "her pack has hunted this land for generations. They will not harm you here. But you should not venture beyond the western tree line until they know you. The pack has no tolerance for strangers."

My mind was a storm of emotion, fear confused by lust, a sense of urgency building to I knew not what. When he moved his hand away from my body, my heart slowed, my legs steadied, I returned, somewhat, to my senses.

"You own a pack of wolves?"

"They cannot be owned. You could call it a mutually beneficial relationship, one built on trust and love. They have been part of my family since before my people came to this land, it is a long and often tragic story."

"That's a story I'd like to hear."

He rested his hand on my chest, and my senses reeled again. I thought my heart would tear itself free from my body and live its last moments in his palm. When his hand moved to my cheek, my blood rushed to meet it. "Not tonight," he said. When he drew his hand away for a second time, a piece of my soul slipped away with it. "I'll return in the morning. I can make you breakfast, then give you a proper tour."

"I'd like that," I whispered through quivering lips.

"I'll see you at dawn," he said, then slid the door aside and walked out. I watched until he and Orla disappeared into the forest. I closed the door, then collapsed face down on the bed, fast asleep.

The next day, I woke before dawn, anticipating Brendan's return. When he didn't arrive with the sun I became annoyed, then felt childish for being angry. He owed me nothing, yet I felt he'd offered more than the promise of breakfast. My agitation grew with the day's light. At length I laughed at myself and thought, "Christopher, you are being foolish."

It was then I noticed the leather jacket. I put it on and walked up to the pool, where I spied a grey stone tower peaking over the trees to the west. I marched down the field, to a breach in the stone boundary wall, and found a path leading deeper into the forest. I walked for half an hour, lost in thought, puzzling over this man under whose spell I'd fallen.

The pack had me surrounded before I realized they were there. They circled, lips curled back, teeth bared, growling and snapping at the air. The circle began to tighten until one of them approached, ears swept back, hackles raised.

I knew it was Orla.

I raised my hands, then held one arm out toward her. "Orla," I said, "I'm a friend, be a good girl and don't eat me, I'm only here to return this to Brendan."

She sniffed the leather, then me. The wet heat of her breath washed over my face. I did my best to avoid her eyes. She moved her snout down the length of my body, then sat in front of me. She turned her head to the sky and let out a deafening howl.

The pack howled with her, the noise grew louder, until a sharp whistle split the air. The pack calmed and moved away while Orla remained seated, blocking the path.

Brendan appeared behind her on the path. He stood next to her and showered her with praise and affection.

"Good girl Orla," he said, several times. When she leaned her body into his, I cringed at my absurd jealousy.

"I warned you Christopher. You're quite fortunate Orla was here."

"You…your coat…you forgot your coat," I stammered.

"It's your uncle's coat" he replied, "it's good you wore it, it has his scent. I'm sorry about this morning, my work took longer than expected. I was on my way to see you. Did you eat without me?"

"I've had coffee."

"You've come this far, walk with me and we'll get you that breakfast."

"I thought I was going to *be* breakfast."

"You still can, if you like," he said.

I laughed but sensed a note of truth in what he said. He slipped his hand into mine and the wolf pack faded into the forest. Again his touch sent me reeling, my heart thumping away. I was certain he could hear it.

"It's nice to have someone to walk with," he said.

I stopped and he turned to face me, but didn't release my hand.

"Brendan, what's happening? This is the most intense seduction. I'm losing myself in someone I don't know. This is..."

"We're meant for each other, a match like no other I've know. I could sense your attraction to me, and mine to you. It is undeniable. I haven't been able to put you out of my mind. I touch you and it's..."

"Overwhelming," I said, "like a boat on a rushing river. I can't stop it, even if I wanted to."

"Then let's embrace this, explore it, find out where it leads us. Something powerful forms between us when we touch, I know you feel it."

I placed his hand against my face, once again my blood raced to meet his touch. When he kissed me I closed my eyes, overtaken by the rush of excitement, the surge of emotion. I knew in that moment he was right.

We resumed our walk and he told me about his people, how they'd been driven from their ancestral land in Ireland early in the 17th century, most of the men killed in battles with the British. They were the last of the Gaelic aristocracy. They searched for safe haven in Spain, then France, where they were granted lands in the east of the country, a place called Colmar. He described its beauty with such detail; the vineyards, the canals, the dry climate. I found myself lost in his memories of wine and gardens, tall mountains, and warm summer winds.

Fifty years later war came to destroy the life they'd made.

His ancestors were uprooted again and fled to Italy. "In Rome," he said, "we regained our strength, our wealth, our power. But my ancestors were finished with the continent. They built a flotilla, loaded all they had aboard the ships, and set sail for the New World. Some of the clan remained in New England, the rest wanted nothing to do with the British. They turned their ships south and settled in places like St. Augustine, New Orleans, some went to islands in the Caribbean, a few to South America."

"That's quite the diaspora," I said.

"Yes," he replied, "And I am the last of my people here. We've developed a liking for warmer climates, but dire wolves aren't built for heat. I stay here to look after the pack, the land, the house."

"It must get lonely."

"At times, in winter. Joey's presence made it less so."

The earthen path transitioned to cobblestones. Great granite walls rose up before us. The lower section had narrow vertical windows cut in the stone. Much larger windows stared down at us from the highest floor. A tower, twenty feet in diameter, rose up above it all and held the only door.

"Welcome to House Cavanagh," he said. He led me into the tower, up a winding staircase to the third floor hall. The inner wall was illuminated by the sunlight streaming in through the windows. Broad wooden planks, worn smooth by ages of use, muffled our footsteps.

An arched window opposite a massive door provided a view to the East. The iron hinges of the door groaned and squealed as it swung inward. A fire blazed within a hearth several feet wide and equally as tall. A plush red sofa sat to the right of the fire. To the left, a colossal bed draped in blue linen occupied a raised a platform. Tapestries hung from the walls, hunting scenes, revelry, an army of knights marching into battle.

"It's old fashioned, but what else could it be?"

"It's fantastic," I said.

"Would you like to sit?" he asked, holding his hand out toward the sofa, smiling softly at me. "Or," he continued, as he moved his hand toward the bed, "would you prefer to lie down?"

We had moved beyond the dance of seduction, I had no intention of turning back. I walked toward the bed and sat on the edge of the thick mattress.

He placed his hand on my chest and gently pushed me down onto the bed. He climbed onto the bed and kissed me.

As our lips came together the air warmed around us, a golden light grew more intense. The light became heat, burning away all I knew, engulfing us in fire. He became something more than human, something beyond my world, a being of energy and heat and shimmering light. He tore at my shirt, I laughed as it came away in smoldering shreds. The inferno subsided, retreating within him. He took my wrists, pinned me to the bed, then looked into my eyes.

"You've had a taste, do you want more? I cannot control myself much longer…"

"Yes," I exhaled.

My head was swimming, I knew what he offered, and I knew my answer.

"Tell me," he said.

"Yes," I said, "I want you, I want it all."

His smile revealed sharp teeth glittering in the light. He plunged them into my chest, delivering exquisite pain exceeded only by the power of the pleasure of his bite. My body was no longer my own. My back arched, pushing against the force of his bite, willing him deeper into my flesh.

"More," I begged.

He raised my arm and wrapped his mouth around my wrist, sank his teeth into my veins and began to drink. My heart threatened to explode from my chest. The fire burned brighter, enveloped us completely, turned my former life to ashes, transformed me into flame. When he was sated, my blood pulsed down my arm, my heart calmed and fell within me, a stone sinking into water. He caressed the wound with his tongue, healing me as if I'd never been torn. He lowered my arm to the bed, then laid his head on my chest, listening to the now faint beating within. He then laid his bare forearm across my lips. "You are mine," he said, "and I will be yours."

Desire swept away inhibition, passion destroyed fear. My teeth tore into him. I drank as man in the desert drinks from the oasis. I took all I could from him, then pulled away, fell back onto the bed, filled my lungs with the flames until the fire was gone. He closed the wound I'd made, then wrapped his arms around my compliant body, whispering words I could not then fathom. I faded in and out of consciousness; time ceased to have any meaning.

When he peeled himself away from me I was weak, but my pulse was steady. Darkness had fallen. He stood at the hearth and stoked the fire. I could not so much as raise my head.

He returned to me and spoke softly, his lips brushing the hair on my chest, "Sleep now," he said. "When you awaken, you will enter a world without pain, without sorrow, without fear; a world beyond anything you can imagine. Sleep now, and dream."

He placed me beneath the blankets, pulled the them up to my chin, and left me to my rest. I lay there, drifting in and out of the world. I dreamt of times I'd never lived, places I'd never been. Eventually I realized I was seeing the world through Brendan's memories, now passed to me. By the time I was strong enough to rise from the bed, I knew him as completely as one could know another, and he knew me equally as well.

On the day of my true awakening, the massive door was

open, the light of a new dawn spilling into the room. I did not know how many days had passed, and I did not care. I rose from my slumber and found Brendan asleep on the sofa. Even immortals need their rest.

I brushed my hand against his cheek, his eyes fluttered open, sparkling green, a smile to greet me. He took my hand and led me from the room. We climbed the winding stair to the top of the tower and stood before the parapet, facing east.

"Now you know me. Do you trust me?"

"What is trust but, love put into action? The word becomes the deed," I replied.

The morning sun shone down from a blue winter sky, banishing the cold, a hint of things to come. I kissed him and felt the now familiar flames engulf us. We rose into the sky, left behind the world of stone and glass, became one with the dawn, and flew together into the arms of eternity.

Ulmarro

I begged my Boss not to send me to Ulmarro. Carried on about it like it was a death sentence. As if a posting there would be the ruin of all I held dear, all I believed, all I wanted from life. And as expected, the bastard sent me there anyway. Yet another data point to prove that I'm not nice, I'm manipulative.

Ulmarro, a tiny planet at the far edge of the known galaxy, its location and size weren't the issue most people took with the place. For most, it was the population. Ninety-seven percent male. You might say it was unique in that regard. It's also considered one of the most dangerous planets in all the galaxy, though no one can ever say exactly why. Something about ultra-violet rays and man-eating plants.

I don't know about any of that, but I do know only one employee, Roger Blakely, the last one sent there by my firm, ever returned. He refused to talk about his experience and resigned his position the day after he made it back to Earth. We hadn't seen hide nor hair of him since. That was a year ago. The post had remained vacant, and the Company was anxious to get another pair of boots, or in my case leather Oxfords, on the ground.

Everyone at the firm went into best-behavior mode when the post at Ulmarro opened up, doing their darnedest to stay on the good side of the Bosses. Unlucky me, I couldn't quite manage good behavior. My name landed on the top of the 'who's next' list within a month of Roger's resignation, and stayed there until the inevitable happened.

When Boss Hampton called me into his office, his Boss, Boss Victoria, was there to back him up. He was a snively little bitch who could never manage the dirty work on his own.

"Mister Summer, I assume you know why you are here."

I didn't respond. He didn't ask a question, so why bother?

"Do you know why we've called you in today?" Boss Victoria asked, already stepping in to keep things from getting too messy.

"I haven't a clue."

"You are aware," Boss Hampton began, "we…I mean the Company, that is, our operation is…"

Boss Victoria couldn't handle the fumbling, and jumped right to the point. "The posting on Ulmarro has been empty too long. We're sending you to fill it. You depart in two weeks."

This is the point in the story where my drama classes paid their dividends. "Why me? Why not Smythington? Or Brownley? Or even Griffiths? He's a cocky bastard, that one, send him."

"There's no cause for foul language," Boss Hampton said, "it won't do any of us proud, now will it?"

"Proud? What do I care about pride? I'm not proud, never have been. In fact, I'll beg if you like. I'll get on my hands and knees and beg, whatever it takes. Please, please, please, don't send me to that god-forsaken place. They say it's dangerous, like, super-danger-planet. Almost nobody comes back, and the ones who do are, well, they're broken, like Blakely. What ever happened to him? He quit, then poof, he disappeared…"

"You're the only bachelor in the building," Boss Victoria said, "and frankly, I think you could use a little time away, some challenge in your life. Perhaps you'll get your head on straight for once, make a better man of you."

"I've got a girlfriend," I said, "what'll I tell her? She's not the type to put her life on hold for me."

"Girlfriend?" Boss Hampton asked. "Since when?"

"Three years, you met her at the Christmas party."

Boss Hampton was incredulous. "That woman was your girlfriend? For the life of me, I thought she was your cousin."

"If she's waited three years for a ring," Boss Victoria said, "she can wait a little longer. The Company can arrange a stasis chamber for her, it's one of your benefits, of course. Although it's normally for spouses, we can make an exception in this case. Really, when she wakes up after you return, it will be as if no time passed at all."

"Boss Victoria, no offense, but what would you know about it? Wait. Two years? The posting is one year. All postings abroad are one year, that's the rule."

"Cost cutting," Boss Hampton said, "with all the inflation of late, we're having to cut back where we can. I'm sure you understand, a fifty percent reduction in travel costs…"

"I most certainly do not understand."

"The decision is made," Boss Victoria said. Her voice rang of finality. "You leave in two weeks, that should be ample time to get your affairs in order. Let the Company know if your *girlfriend* wants to take the Big Sleep while you're away."

I knew there was no way out, but I laid it on thick anyway, in hopes of making them feel bad, or at a minimum, pissing them off. I didn't care, I wouldn't see them again, what did it matter? Between the travel time across the galaxy and the two years on station, I'd be gone for 100-plus years. These people were about to be dead to me.

"Can I at least have the rest of the day off?"

They looked at each other and smiled, then turned back to me.

"Of course you may," Boss Hampton said.

"In fact," Boss Victoria added, "why don't you consider yourself on paid leave until your departure, take some time to properly prepare yourself for the journey ahead."

"I will," I replied, "I most certainly will."

I gathered my few personal belongings from my desk and made my way out of the building. All of my fellow actuaries avoided eye contact with me as I walked through our open-floor-plan office space, but I swear I heard someone whisper, 'better him than me, poor bastard.'

If only he knew.

I tossed my junk into the frunk and hopped into my auto-auto, set the destination for home, and dialed up 'that woman.'

"Jonny, it's been months, to what do I owe the pleasure of your call?"

"I'm shipping out, Betty, they're sending me to Ulmarro in two weeks, even gave me a paid vacation until the departure."

"It only took you three years, well done. I'm happy for you Jonny, I can't wait to tell your brother. He'll want to celebrate, of course. And why shouldn't we? When will we see you?"

"I think the Christmas party sealed the deal. Once they thought I had someone special in my life, it was all but over for me. Sadistic bastards. How about tonight?"

"Tonight is too soon, tomorrow is better. Are you saying your sister-in-law is not special to you?"

"No, not at all…I mean, that's not what I'm saying. You're definitely special…"

I stopped talking when I heard her laughing. We'd been best friends since college. We met in my first drama class and became like peas in a pod. It made sense my brother liked her too. They married two months after she graduated, but that never got in the way of her being my 'date' for corporate events.

You see, in the insurance business, particularly the life insurance business, everyone must have someone or some institution about which they care enough to fork over hard-earned money every month to maintain a financial instrument from which they will derive exactly zero return. That statement is practically the Company moto. Not the public motto, but the motto they use to encourage laggard policy salespeople to make their quotas.

If they thought I was a sad-sack loner, or worse, a confirmed bachelor with no sanctioned attachments, I would have never made it to Senior Actuary. I had to get the promotion, then I had to give them a reason to send me to the most remote office in the Company, and I had to make them think I had something, or someone, to lose. They only felt good about being cruel to someone they thought deserved it, and what's more cruel than separating someone from their loved ones for a century or two?

But I didn't care about any of that anymore. What mattered to me was getting a get a free ride to the most distant planet in the known galaxy. With any luck, my laser-gram to Freddy would make it to Ulmarro ahead of his arrival.

He shipped out four years ago, leaving him another century or so in the Big Sleep, with a few years on the far end to wait for me once he got there. He'd wake up as young and handsome as he was the day his Company shipped him off, and meet me at the spaceport on Ulmarro with bells on once I made the trip.

A few years on Ulmarro without me, I'm sure he'd find ways to fill his time. Didn't matter to me what he got into, as long as he was there for me when I caught up to him.

No civilian can afford the price of a pan-galactic ticket. But to a life insurance company, with a vested interest in having a Company actuary onsite wherever they do business, and a private fleet of interstellar spacecraft, the cost barely warrants a line item in the financial statement, Boss Hampton's comments about budgets aside.

My years-long plan was at last coming to fruition. I redirected my car to a Galactic Union office, fired off the laser-gram to Freddy, and boot-scooted back to my condo to get my accounts in order. You can't transfer money across space, but you can transfer it to a ship-board account and have it all with you when you arrive. Being an actuary pays well, but I lived like a pauper.

I'd been saving every credit I could, and earning as much extra as possible by opening my car up for self-driven ride shares, renting out my walk-in closet to a politician from out of state, and bartending at the city's most popular dance club on weekends. I'm a shit bartender, but the joint ran on volume, not quality.

When I got home, Representative Marcus stepped out of the shower and started toweling off in my bedroom. Straight as an arrow, pure as the driven snow, neither of those characteristics stopped him from being a tease ever since he moved into my closet. I often wondered if his wife knew the full truth about his living arrangements.

"Looking good Congressman, looking good," I cooed.

"Thank you, Jonny, I do my best to stay in shape," he replied as he dried his not-quite-private regions. "They say this job will add ten pounds per year to your weight, and take ten years off your life at the same time. I can't afford either."

He tossed the towel into my laundry bin and helped himself to a pair of my favorite briefs from my dresser. "Hope you don't mind," he said, "haven't had a chance to do my laundry this week."

"By all means, help yourself, or you could go without for the rest of the night."

"No can do, as attractive as the notion may be. I'll be out for the evening, you'll be all by your lonesome for dinner." He slipped into my underwear and said, "What's with the box, did you get fired?"

Of course he would be concerned. No job, no condo, no condo, no closet for him to live in.

"No," I replied, "I've been posted to the Ulmarro office, I leave in two weeks."

"Two weeks.... Jonny, there's no possibility I can find suitable lodging in two weeks. You know I'm not made of money, I can't..."

"Take it easy big boy, you're not going anywhere. After I leave, you can have the whole place to yourself for as long as you need it. Same rent, but you'll send it to my brother. How's that sound?"

"Sounds too good to be true. The whole place, an entire one-bedroom condo, all for me, at today's rates. Is there a catch? As comfortable as I am with your man-on-man lifestyle, you know, it's not for me, I..."

"Do you want there to be a catch?" I asked.

To my surprise, he actually thought about for a hot second.

"Ummm, no. No, I do not. Thank you, Jonny, quite generous. But you know I'm a terrible liar. What with the ongoing purge of...people like you...I couldn't risk the dalliance. One question, and I'd give myself up, couldn't possibly risk it. You know my party, we're the opposition, we don't pull the strings these days. But I'll miss you all the same, you know. We should celebrate, you've been chasing this posting for years. What say we have dinner and drinks at my club tomorrow evening?"

"No can do, already have plans tomorrow. You have a club? Is it men only? How can you afford it? How about Thursday?"

"Yes, doesn't everyone? Of course it's men-only, strictly enforced. And I don't pay for my membership, as long as I'm in office. Thursday won't do. We'll figure something out, two weeks you said? Plenty of time."

Two weeks was not plenty of time. After our conversation, the Honorable Representative Marcus went to the roof to meet his taxi and flew off to the Capital Building. We barely saw each other after that. Probably for the best.

The Gay Purge had been in full swing for the better part of a decade. It was a terrible time. Centuries of cultural advancement, wiped out, along with most of the rest of the Constitution. It was a good time to have a Congressman living in your closet; investigations of elected officials, regardless of party, were strictly illegal. No one crossed that line.

The two weeks flew by, and before I knew it, I was at the spaceport ready to board my ship and start my journey to a better a life, albeit a life most people would view as far worse than my current one.

My brother and his wife were there to see me off, but the presence of Company personnel made for an odd presentation. We had to keep up appearances right until the end. I kissed my sister-in-law, on the lips no less, then shook my brother's hand. When he started blubbering, and she started giggling, I knew it was time to go.

I wish I could say the trip was exciting and eventful, but it was neither. They put you down for the Big Sleep before launch, which eliminated the need for things like windows and private quarters, and kept all the passengers blissfully unaware in the event of a launch failure.

My particular flight was a 'ride share' launch. Two dozen passengers, each in their own smaller, single-person ship, went up on one big booster. We'd all get released into space, then get shoved through a warp-bubble generator and fly away to our individual destinations. If I thought about it too much, I'd be terrified, so I avoided thinking about being all alone in a tiny vessel zipping across space for a hundred years.

Now that I think of it, it wasn't much more dangerous than being homosexual in the age of purges and hate-filled speeches. Plus, I'd be asleep until I arrived at my destination.

I wouldn't know if anything bad happened, any more than I would know if the launch failed.

I got fitted into my sleeping suit, plugged into my compartment, and boom, out went the lights. When I next became aware of my own existence, I thought something must have gone wrong. It seemed as though a few seconds had passed and suddenly I was being told by the onboard computer that I was docking at Ulmarro. When I tried to lift my hand to rub my eyes, I knew then I'd been down for a long trip. I couldn't do it, couldn't lift my own hand. Too weak. No one warned me about this part of the adventure. Oops.

My tiny vessel docked with the orbital station, a slight bump, some metal-on-metal squealing and squeaking, and I had arrived. Despite my physical state, I was thrilled to be one step closer to Freddy.

Then, nothing happened.

That's not entirely correct. Lights came on inside my one-person ship, but after that, nothing. I waited for what I felt was a reasonable amount of time before I started screaming. I doubt anyone could hear me, but once I wore myself out, I felt better. I eventually fell asleep, which was a strange thing to do after sleeping for over a century, but that's what happened.

I didn't wake up until a voice said, "Standby for intramuscular stimulation."

This, if I'm being honest, sounded like fun when I heard it. But no, it was not fun. Needles flipped out from little ports over my legs, chest and arms. They primed themselves, then all at once every one of them stabbed me and started pumping away. It hurt like hell and, yes, I started screaming again.

Within a few seconds the pain mysteriously vanished. I can't explain it, but I can theorize. I think perhaps the initial injection, the first drip of the poke, contained pain killers or numbing agents. Because after the first shocking assault, I started feeling good. More than good, I felt great. It was as if my soft tissue was being rebuilt and reshaped all over and within my body. Small devices joined their needle brethren and began massaging and kneading my ancient flesh, bringing it back to life again, restoring my body.

When the needles retracted and the massaging stopped, I found I missed their touch and was hoping there was a second phase of the process. No such luck. As soon as I could move again, the front of my ship opened and a voice from an overhead speaker said, "Welcome to Ulmarro Station, Mister Summer, please follow the white line to the arrival desk for check-in."

I stepped out of my vessel and into a narrow corridor, wearing only my thong-sized 'sleeping suit,' and a foolish grin.

I scanned my resurrected body. I looked great. My body was in better shape than when I left Earth, thanks to all those needles and drugs and massaging bots. I had the physique of a middle-weight prize fighter. But that suit was skimpy, and I was close to falling out of it.

I didn't see anyone else around. I picked up my lone bag and asked the speaker in the ceiling, "What about my clothes? Where can I change out of this suit?"

"Welcome to Ulmarro Station Mister Summer, please follow the white line to the arrival desk for check-in."

"Okay then, I'll follow the white line and whoever is there to meet me can get the full view of all my bits and baubles."

The white line consisted of a series of glowing white lights embedded in the floor. The floor curved up and away from me. I'd seen images of the orbital station and knew the docking ports were situated along the outer edge of a spinning space wheel.

It's spinning simulated Earth gravity, which was fine until I started walking and felt like I was going uphill the entire way. All my newly pumped muscles needed more oxygen than my lungs and heart could deliver, having been at rest for a century.

I made it to the reception desk on the verge of collapse.

The android attached to the desk, *bolted* to the top of it, in the same voice I'd heard previously, said, "Welcome to Ulmarro Station Mister Summer, your documents please." It pointed a metallic finger at a scanner embedded in the desktop, and waited.

I looked around to make sure I was still the only human in sight. "You need documents? After an interstellar flight? You think I'm a stowaway or something? I flew a private ship across the vastness of space and managed to arrive safe and sound, and you want to see my documentation?"

"Welcome to Ulmarro Station Mister Summer, your documents please."

"Where can I change into some proper clothing?"

"Welcome to Ulmarro Station Mister Summer, your documents please."

"When was the last time someone tried to sneak into Ulmarro from a private spacecraft?"

"Welcome to Ulmarro *Station* Mister Summer, your documents please."

"For the love of Pete, fine, my documents," I said and slapped my hand onto the scanner.

Nothing happened and the android repeated, "Welcome to Ulmarro Station Mister Summer, your *documents* please."

"My bio-signature is the only document I have. What else could you want? No, don't say anything, give me a minute to think."

The android stared at me with its expressionless metal face and dim glowing eyes, hand held out, finger frozen over the scanner. I considered walking away, but had no idea where I could go. Then I remembered, the Company had sent me an envelope in the days prior to my departure. An envelop I never bothered to open.

I rummaged about in my bag until I found it, crumpled up in the bottom like a discarded tissue. Paper was largely a thing of the past on Earth, but the station had been built at a time when people still carried things like ID cards and passports. I tore open the envelope and found a single sheet of paper with an EZ-Code printed in the center. A seemingly random collection of dots and blocks inside a two-inch circle of red, I placed it on the scanner and did my best to smooth it out.

"Scan failed," the android said, "please try again, or come back later."

"Come back later? Where would I go to come back from?"

"Scan failed," the android repeated, "please try again, or come back later."

"We should never have banned AI," I grumbled as I lifted the paper off the scanner and began sliding it back and forth over the edge of the desk in an effort to smooth out more wrinkles. I placed it back on the glass surface and held my palm down over the center.

"Scan complete, please follow the green line to changing room number one."

I stuffed the paper in my bag and followed the green lights to a door that slid into the wall when I stopped in front of it. The room was bare, save for a curved seat protruding from the wall. The door closed behind me and the walls became mirrors. I took a moment to look over my body, pleased with the results of my reanimation.

"Freddy's gonna like this," I said to my reflection.

I peeled away the skimpy sleeping suit and a chute opened in the wall next to the seat. I dropped the suit in, the door closed, followed by a loud "swooshing" sound. I imagined the bit of fabric and wiring being ejected into space, where it would fall toward the planet and burn up in the atmosphere. I also imagined thousands upon thousands of stinking little sleeping suits drifting in orbit, bumping into each other, sometimes sticking together, possibly forming new lifeforms, at which point I decided to put it out of my mind all together.

Sadly, the stink didn't leave the room with the suit, and it occurred to me I didn't want to dress without bathing first. No sooner had I thought the thought than a panel in the wall slid aside, revealing a chamber with nozzles of varying configuration sticking out of the walls, but no obvious means of control.

I stepped into the chamber, the panel closed behind me, the lights dimmed, and soft music began to play.

"This is nice," I said to myself. Then a viscous liquid, ice cold, started squirt out from tubes all around, pelting me from all directions with its slimy frigidness. It set my heart racing and I wanted to cry out but didn't dare for fear of getting the liquid in my mouth. It was already burning my eyes and filling my ears, where it congealed and plunged me into near total silence. I tried to open the panel to retreat from the onslaught, to no avail. Everything was coated in slippery slime, a cold as ice. I sat on the floor and braced my back against the wall to try to kick the panel open, when the squirting came to an abrupt stop.

I stood and tensed up, waiting for whatever came next. In the silent dim chamber, my eyes burning like fire, I began to feel a strange sensation all over my body. The slimy liquid began to foam, and the foam began to roam about my body, seeking out all the hidden places the liquid had not reached. I began to burn in other places, especially my nether regions. The burning was becoming unbearable in those places when suddenly the lights went up and water, warm wonderful water, came jetting out of the nozzles. The foam was soon gone, and with it the burning and the horrible sensation of millions of tiny creatures crawling all over me, eating away the scum of my deep space deep sleep.

The water cleansed my eyes, my ears, eradicated the foam from every nook and cranny. It wasn't long before I could hear the music again, but the tune changed to some kind of ancient music, with high-pitched stringed instruments and clanging brass. There was singing too, but I couldn't understand a word of it. It was a jaunty number, I'll give it that.

When it ended, the water jets were replaced by alternating currents of hot and cold air, buffeting and swirling around me. I was dry in less than a minute, but the air kept moving, until it was spinning like a miniature hurricane around my head.

Then another odd sensation, this time concentrated on my head. Little pricks of pain, growing in intensity and frequency. I noticed something floating down from the maelstrom around my skull and realized it was my own hair.

"No," I shouted, "stop it, I like my hair."

But it didn't stop. Not until it was finished. The air stopped spinning around my head and the whirling currents split into cyclones, blasting away any cut hair that dared cling to me. By then I had surrender to the process. Which was not entirely useful since the process was complete.

The panel opened, releasing me to the mirrored room, where I was shocked to discover my new hair cut looked good, as did the other places where excess growth had been trimmed. I stared at myself for a few minutes, impressed by the results.

"Not bad for old tech," I said, then opened my bag and picked out what I thought would be an appropriate outfit for my reunion with Freddy.

Unfortunately, when I went to the vestibule near the desk-droid station, Freddy wasn't there to greet me. Instead, I was met by a Company Man, with a dossier.

He held a thin plastic file folder out toward me, "You're onboarding package Mister Summer," he said.

"You couldn't give this to me on the surface?"

"My job here is finished. I'm taking your transport to my next assignment. I never go planet-side, not in my job description."

"You mean it's above your pay grade?"

"More like below, but it's not a competition, is it? Enjoy your time on Ulmarro, I hear the beaches are nice. Hard to get to, dangerous tides, and you can't go in the water, but nice all the same."

Typical Company craziness. Pinch pennies at every opportunity, then spend a fortune flying some poor slob around the galaxy to hand out notebooks and ID badges. Then again, whatever they were paying him, he was earning it.

Centuries upon centuries in stasis, bouncing around the galaxy to hand out little dossiers to people he'd never see again. I mean, either he loved his alone time, or whoever loved him didn't mind waiting out his travels in stasis back on Earth. A Big Sleep bigger than any other Big Sleep. It was too depressing to think about, which helped me stop thinking about it.

The Company Man started walking away, back the way I had come. "Wait, I have questions," I called after him.

"Everything you need is in your hands."

"What about transportation?"

"It's in there."

"Where is my office?"

"It's all in there, take a look," he tossed over his shoulder.

"When's my first day?"

He didn't look back, didn't reply. The last thing I saw him do before he rounded the corner was raise his right hand and point his middle finger in the air. The ancient and universal sign for "have a nice day."

"Great, not planet-side yet, and I've already got homework."

The same android voice spoke from the ceiling again, "Welcome procedure complete. Please follow the blue line to the Central Hub. Your shuttle will depart in nine minutes, twenty-two seconds."

I stuffed the dossier into my bag and followed the blue lights in the floor toward the Central Hub, the zero-gravity cylinder at the center of the station.

I had no idea how long it would take me to get to the shuttle bay, and I had no intention of missing the drop. I was moving quickly, eyes down at the floor, following a maddening set of turns and branches in my path. I can be forgiven for not realize I wasn't alone anymore.

I arrived at yet another android desk, where I was once again asked to scan my EZ-Code. It took a few tries, which led to an audible 'harumph' from behind me. I turned back and discovered there was a line of men behind me, all about my age, all nicely dressed, with trim builds and what appeared to be exactly the same haircut as mine. I counted four, before the line turned a corner, hiding its true nature from me.

"Sorry," I said to the assumed harumpher.

"Perhaps someone could help you," he said, with a tone that made it clear he had no interest in being helpful.

"No," I said, "I got this." And on the fourth attempt, I did get it.

"Please proceed to exit portal Alpha-3," the desk droid said. "Next."

I stepped around the desk and it wasn't until I was

standing at my designated portal that I asked myself: "Where the hell am I going?"

I dragged my onboarding dossier out of my bag and opened it. There was one piece of paper inside, printed on both sides. As far as I knew, there were three major cities on the planet, cleverly named after cities on Earth - New Chicago, New Dallas, and New Boston.

I wasn't concerned about which city I landed in, as long as it wasn't New Chicago, the agricultural center of Ulmarro, or New Dallas, the energy producing heartland of the planet. They were fine cities, in their own way, but they were each several days away from Freddy. New Boston was the financial and cultural center, and that suited me.

Once I was down, no matter which city I was assigned to, I would make my home in New Boston, with Freddy. If I had to, I would set up a robo-proxy, with remote login, in my official office to make it look like I was there, whether I was or not.

Fortunately, my dossier informed me I was assigned to an office in the heart of New Boston. Whether you could swim in it or not, Freddy and I always wanted to live near the ocean, because looking at the ocean is the next best thing to frolicking in it, we agreed.

Freddy. My Freddy. My secret elicit-love-affair Freddy. He was an actuary, like me, but worked for a different Company. I would say competing Company, but really, no one competing in business anymore. The world ran on winks and nods and closed-door deals, which didn't do much for the everyday people of the world, but did wonders for corporate balance sheets.

Freddy had a side-hustle, working as a lobbyist in the Capital, until he decided to do the bang-bang with a Congressman in his Capital office and, oops, they got caught by an intern. True story, the intern is a Senator now, and the

Congressman is back on the farm, or wherever it is he started out his life.

Nobody wanted the scandal, and nobody got one, but the little affair was the final straw for Freddy's Company. It was all they needed to ship him out to Ulmarro. The Company already had it in for Freddy over one untimely, but rather large, mistake in a risk assessment (more on that later).

We'd been dating a year at that point and were ready to 'make it official' in a secret ceremony with an illegal marriage, and yes, I did forgive him for his little fling. It's business, after all, and we all want to get ahead, am I right?

A light went on over my portal and a series of 'dings' sounded down the line and around the outwardly curved wall of the shuttle bay. The shuttle wasn't exactly one ship. It was more a collection of small pods, each independent, like escape pods, and interconnected through a primary framework.

The shuttle would fly over each city, spit out the appropriate pods, and fly back to the station. The pods would get collected later, flown back up to the station together, and stand ready for the next batch of arrivals, which could happen in a year, a century, or never again.

As an aside, this drop-and-go design scheme had an extra benefit. If something were to go wrong, and the shuttle was in danger of crashing, all the pods could be jettisoned, and hopefully somebody would survive. A rather thoughtful bit of engineering, I'd say.

I snuggled into my pod, the door closed behind me, and a voice, human-sounding this time, announced, "This is your pilot, Captain Nelly Anderson. On behalf of the crew and all of us here at Transplanetary Transportation Services, I'd like to welcome you all aboard. We'll be departing momentarily. Your personalized flight and destination information is displayed on the screen to your left, entertainment options are available on the screen to your right. Now, sit back, relax, and enjoy your flight."

The view screen embedded in the pod door flickered to life and displayed my destination, New Boston, and a flight time of 51 minutes and 44 seconds, with an on-time percentage of - surprise, surprise - 100 percent. And a 'JA' of '42Kkm,' whatever that was. I tapped the right screen, pulled up the music app, and tapped 'Random.'

Why 'Random?' Because I know myself and I know I could spend the entire flight trying to figure out what to play. Why not let a computer do it for me?

The screen flickered and something called the '1812 Overture' began to play. It had a runtime of 16 minutes, which was perfect for me. It started out quiet and gentle, some kind of wind instruments. I started to dose off, until I was jolted wide awake when I remember 'JA' stood for 'Jettison Altitude' and '42Kkm' meant I would be shot from the shuttle an altitude of 42000 kilometers.

It had to be a mistake. There's no way a small pod could carry enough fuel to land safely from that altitude. My heart was racing, I could feel stress-sweat forming all over my body. Right when I was trying to calm myself, the music took on this insane sense of urgency and energy. Cymbals started crashing, bells started tolling, and to my abject horror, explosions! The music had explosions in it! I made a mental note to one day find out what the hell happened in 1812, if I survived my landing.

"Computer, can you hear me? Are you there?"

"Audio interface activated. How may I be of assistance?"

"Describe landing procedure."

"This shuttle does not land."

"Not the shuttle, *me,* how do *I* land in New Boston? What's the process?"

'The landing procedure for drop-pods is fully automated,

there is nothing for you to do. Please relax and enjoy your flight."

"No!" I shouted, then tried to calm myself with a few deep breaths. "Computer, describe for me how this pod I'm in, will leave this shuttle it is on, and deliver me safely to New Boston."

"Understood," the computer replied, "The drop-pod you occupy will be jettisoned from the shuttle at an altitude of forty-two-thousand kilometers, or approximately twenty-six thousand miles, for those still using the Archaic System. The pod will free-fall to an altitude of eight thousand kilometers, approximately five thousand miles."

"You can stop with the Archaic nonsense, when was the last time anyone used it?"

"The phrase 'last time' adds a level of complexity to any response. Time, being relative to you, the planet, the colony, Earth, and my encoded system, requires a rather lengthy set of possible answers, beginning with time in the context of the founding of the Ulmarro Colony."

"No," I shouted, then more quietly, "Please, let's move on."

"Very well. At an altitude of eight thousand kilometers, primary retro rockets will fire, slowing the pod to one thousand kilometers per minute. This will be a very exciting time during your descent. You may wish to open your portal cover to fully appreciate the experience. At one thousand kilometers, secondary retro rockets should fire, slowing your descent to a manageable one hundred kilometers per minute. If secondary ignition is successful, landing parachutes should deploy within fifteen seconds, further slowing…"

I felt my hair stand on end, and I began screaming, as I had when I woke up in my transport pod, "Wait! What do you mean, '*should*' what happens '*if not*'?" What are my odds? Am I gonna die? What kind of system is this?"

"Systems detect a dangerous heart rate and blood pressure

reading indicating you are in hypertensive crisis. Deploying countermeasures."

"Stop!" No! What's happening *now*?"

A pale mist filled the pod. I tried not to breathe it, but there was no hope. I couldn't hold my breath, largely due to the fact I couldn't catch it. I sucked in a lung-full of the mist. Despite my circumstances, I felt an intense warm wave of calm wash over me. 'I die,' I thought, 'at least I'll die at peace.'

"You seem to be feeling better," the computer said, "would you like me to continue with your landing sequence description?"

"No," I said, "no, I'm good. All good." And I was. I felt more at ease than I'd felt in ages. "Sooooo good," I sighed, then passed out.

And I dreamt of a place long gone from earth, a place Freddy and I had visited once, before the ocean rose and wiped it from the face of the earth. A place called 'Provincetown.' The very place that got Freddy shipped out to Ulmarro.

A little history for those who skipped it - Provincetown was a tiny little fishing village, the first place a bunch of religious fanatics landed on the continent once called 'North America.' They landed there, fleeing persecution for being the zealots everyone claimed they were, and, in their wisdom, decided to move on.

They'd landed on the outer tip of a place later called 'Cape Cod,' (until it wasn't a cape anymore and was renamed 'Cod Shoals'), and discovered they couldn't make a go of it there. Too sandy to grow crops, too bereft of animals they could eat, and far too pretty for a group of people who prided themselves on their commitment to austerity, self-flagellation, and righteous indignation.

Too bad they weren't skilled at fishing, the entire world

might have turned out different.

Some time later, some other settlers came along, ones who *could* fish, and they built, what else, a fishing village. And they did okay. Not great, but okay.

Then the gays showed up. And the gays changed everything. Provincetown became, and for centuries remained, a kind of Mecca for all the colors of the same-sex, alt-sex, or non-binary rainbow. Alas, it did not last. What the purges didn't destroy, the rising tides wiped away, or left in ruins.

But we, Freddy and I, got to spend one glorious week there before it all ended. We stayed in an inn on a bluff with a stunning view of the harbor and the adjacent salt marsh. We spent hours on the sandy beaches, occasionally dipping our toes into the ocean (there were rules, even then, about how much of your body you could expose in public), and evenings dining at local eateries and shopping for art we couldn't, or wouldn't, afford. It was blissful beyond belief. We were devastated when it all washed away.

It was worse for Freddy, he was *there* when it happened. Can you imagine? You show up to do a risk assessment to revise your tables and increase your insurance rates and *swoosh,* it's all gone, in the blink of an eye, as they say. Ultimately, it's why Freddy got shipped out to Ulmarro. Apparently, given his job, he was supposed to be able to predict the future. It wasn't his fault a tsunami hit before he could raise rates and cancel policies. Who knew there were earthquakes in New England?

He held on to his gig as long as he could, but eventually caved to the pressure after getting busted for that little fling I mentioned earlier. They offered him a choice: Take the assignment or suffer the double humiliation of being fired for cause and being publicly outed. He took the assignment.

But not before concocting a plan to get me there too.

I mean, it's the most dangerous planet know to humanity, but wouldn't you rather face such a place with your beloved, rather then let them face it alone.

I guess most people would say 'no' to that, but if you're Freddy and me, living our clandestine life in the age of purges and hate, you kind of see it - imminent danger - the way you see time. A relative sort of thing.

Enough history, back to my dream. It's more interesting.

There was this place in Provincetown where a guy played piano and sang all sorts of songs. He was great. A kid from Berklee or maybe Juilliard, or some such musically-focused educational institution which, though excellent at turning out well-rounded musicians, didn't really do much for the broader economy anymore. I mean, if they did, why was this virtuoso playing piano at a bar in an old inn? You tell me.

Nevertheless, the way it worked was, you go up and drop 5 or 10 or 50 dollars in one jar on the piano, and in the other jar you drop a slip of paper with the name of the song you were requesting.

I dreamt of the evening Freddy and I spent there, sipping expensive cocktails, listening to one fun, or sad, or melancholy, song after another, and I said, "Wouldn't it be fun if he played a classic, something from that gal….what was her name? She lived to be like, 112 years old, you know the one."

Freddy raised an eyebrow and grinned, "You mean Cher?"

Freddy did love the classics.

"Yes," I said, excited, "that's the one, she had a song. I think it was some kind of breakup revenge song, but upbeat, we danced to it at your place one night."

"I know the song you're thinking of," he said, smiling sweetly, "but I don't think he can play it."

"Sure he can," I said, waving my hand at the piano player, "he can play anything, he'll figure it out."

And in my dream Freddy leaned over, kissed me, and said, "Anything for you babe."

Or maybe he stood up and said, "Okay, here goes nothing."

I like the first version better. In my dream he kissed me, called me 'babe,' scribbled on a piece of paper, then showed it to me.

And I smiled up at him and said, "Yes, my love, that's the one."

Call it saccharine if you want, it's still a sweet moment.

Freddy stuffed the slip into the slip jar, then stuffed a hundred credit note into the tip jar, and boy did that get the piano player's attention. For perspective, because money is like danger, and requires some perspective to truly understand, a hundred credits would cover two nights at our inn. It was a bit extravagant, but Freddy earned a lot more than me. Good on him for splurging a little.

We waited with gleeful anticipation for our song to come up, holding hands under the table, ordering another round of drinks and a nacho platter to keep from getting too drunk.

And we waited some more. We waited long enough to consider ordering another nacho platter.

But then, like a miracle, our song got picked. I mean it should, for a hundred credits.

The piano player pulled the slip from the jar, looked around, and to a now hushed audience says, "Believe, by Cher." A collective gasp followed. Everyone knew it was on the banned song list. A hubbub erupted as a several patrons headed for the exit.

But we didn't move. We held our breath and waited to see what happened.

The piano player scanned the entire room and landed on Freddy and me. "I won't ask who requested this one," he said, "but I will say, thank you. It's a great song, I've always wanted to play this one. In truth, I've dreamt of how I would do it, ever since I downloaded a version of it from the Banned Songs Archive at my school. I hope you like my take on it."

We were feeling awesome because it seemed the size of Freddy's tip mattered, not only to me and the piano player, but to everyone who stuck around to hear the song. It felt magical, sitting there in the low light, fresh drinks on our table, holding hands, surrounded by people *like us,* people willing to risk prison and possible torture and dismemberment for listening to a banned song. Truly magical.

The piano player started with a simple note, let it hang in the air, then another, then one more, then a slight flourish, and finally his voice rose from almost a whisper to a beautiful, room-filling falsetto, "No matter how hard I try...,"

He sang in a way I can only describe as mournfully soulful, or maybe soulfully mournful. Either way, I began to cry. Crying to a banned song was considered an 'aggravating circumstance,' but I was all-in.

I felt Freddy squeeze my hands. I'd been staring at the piano player, but Freddy kept his eyes on me. I turned to face him, saw that sweet smile on his face, and said, "I'll never leave you Freddy, I promise I."

"I know," he replied, "and I'll never let you go. And you'll cross a galaxy to to find me again, and I'll be waiting for you Jonny, waiting for you to wake up, and rejoin the living."

Imagine at this point my dream is interrupted by the sound of screeching tires on an out-of-control auto-auto about to slam into a hapless pedestrian crossing against the light. Imagine it, because that's how I suddenly felt. Rather jarring.

But the feeling passed, thankfully.

What followed was a warm sensation all over. Then a waft of fresh air, something sweet adrift on the wind, a gentle hand on my face, a voice softly urging, "Wake up Jonny. Time to wake up now."

My eyes fluttered open and I thought I was still dreaming. Freddy was kneeling next to me, hand on my cheek, smiling down at me. He looked exactly as I remembered him; tall, lean, a shock of close-cropped black hair, bright blue eyes. Handsome doesn't do him justice.

Still strapped into my now-open pod I ask, "Is this real? It can't be real."

"Yeah, babe, it's real. I hope you like the dream engram. I made it myself, had it coded into your pod. You almost missed it, you pushy little man."

"What...wha...," I tried to sit up.

"Relax, Jonny," Freddy said, "give it another minute for the sleepy drugs to wear off. Can you be still for a minute?"

"Maybe."

"That's my Jonny," he said. He moved his hand to my chest, "You're heart rate seems good," he said, looking at a small screen inside the pod, "respiration too. We'll have you up and dancing in no time."

"Freddy, the dream, a lot of it was..."

"Real? A memory? Did you like it? I made a few last-minute tweaks, but I think they worked."

"Yeah, yeah they did but..."

"I'll explain everything soon. For now, all you need to know is I've been watching you from the moment you arrived in orbit until right now, and I'm never taking my eyes off you again. How do you feel about that?"

I looked beyond his handsome face, stared at the blood-red clouds against the deep azure sky, smelled the ocean on the breeze, then looked into his eyes and said, "I didn't cross the galaxy for a one-nighter. You're stuck with me mister. But how..."

"The dream? Encoding the pod was easy. Once they drop, they get packed into a launcher and shot back up to the station. But getting you into the right pod, that was the tricky part. Luckily, the Company Man that met you on the station is sympathetic, an ally, and you might say a romantic sort."

"*That* guy? You could have fooled me."

"He had to hurry, and make you hurry. I needed you in exactly the right spot in line to get you into exactly the right pod."

"That's a lot of effort for a dream."

"Not for the dream silly goose, for the drop zone. The dream was a bonus feature. I wanted you here, with me. The city is too far away. Your office there is all set, by the way, the bots can handle everything, you can work from here. You can travel anywhere from here, if you need to, but probably won't need to. It's all been arranged. I've had lots of time on my hands, waiting for you. Time to plan."

"Plan? Plan what?"

Freddy laughed, then looked all around, then down at me, "Feel like getting out of this coffin now?"

"Yes, absolutely," I replied, and started to sit up.

Freddy took my hand and helped me rise and step out of the pod. When I felt stable on my feet I surveyed my surroundings. What I saw felt shockingly familiar. Like I'd seen it all before. No, like I'd *been there* before.

We were in a small park in the middle of a roundabout. Other pods had landed around mine. Other couples were in the process of reuniting. A bluff rose up behind us. In front of us, a breakwater made of enormous angular stones, some as large as my auto-auto, stretched out toward distant dunes. To its left, the harbor, high tide lapping at the crest of the wall. To its right, a vast marsh. Tall reeds danced in the light wind and clear water rushed around them. The light of the two setting suns of Ulmarro bathed the scene in a kaleidoscope of color.

I looked up at the bluff, then my eyes followed the road

running along its base. In the distance I could see a stone tower rising up to the sky, a parapet at its peak. I recognized it immediately as Pilgrim Monument.

I looked back at Freddy in disbelief. "How is this possible?"

Freddy smiled, took, both of my hands, and kissed me gently on the lips. Our first kiss in over a century, "Welcome to New Provincetown," he said. "How do you like it so far?"

"So far? So far I like it very much, but how…"

"It wasn't easy," he said, "but a group of us, we saw the writing on the wall and we cooked up this crazy idea. We picked up the entire town, had it shipped out here. Every rock, tree, bucket of sand, art gallery, restaurant, inn, you name it, we sent it all, even some of the locals."

"How…what…who paid for it?"

"The Company, of course, who else could afford it? We leveraged the whole transaction, a lot of creative accounting went into it. I can explain later if you're interested. Once the town was declared a disaster zone, we routed the insurance money where it needed to go to pay off the debt. But the town was already here long before that happened."

"When? I don't understand the timeline. We were there, Freddy, together, we were *there*."

"Not exactly," he said, "I made your dream seem like a dream version of a memory. I never got to take you there, we never spent a week on the beach, at the inn, none of it. But I wanted you to know what it *could* be like, what I hoped it *would* be like, if we were there together."

The world began to spin around me, my eyes fluttered and I became dizzy, nauseous. "You're saying my memories, in the dream, and the dream, they're not real, but this is real, and I know this place, but it's not *this* place I know, and I've never been to *that* place in the first place…"

I collapsed into his arms and the world grew dim. The last

thing I heard was Freddy's voice.

"It's okay Jonny, it happens all the time, it's okay, a little case of intergalactic dissonance, you'll be fine, you'll be fine."

Then it was fine, relatively speaking.

I woke up in a large bed, soft sheets and plump pillows, perfect temperature and the perfect amount of humidity. The lights were off. The room was bathed in green-blue light flowing in through a glass wall.

I sat up and looked out at the marsh below, an entirely new kaleidoscope presented itself, this time created by Ulmarro's three moons. It stretched out from the base of the bluff and disappeared beyond the horizon.

I was in a home I recalled, or had been implanted with the memory of, from our dream trip, but not real trip, to Provincetown. I remember seeing the house on the bluff, pointing up at it and saying to Freddy, "If I could live here, I'd want to live *there*." The recollection made me dizzy again and I laid back down.

I heard a door slide open, quiet footsteps across a thick carpet, then Freddy sat on the edge of the bed, looking down at me.

He smiled, as he had when I'd awakened in the pod, "Feeling better?" he asked.

"No, not really," I replied.

"Give it some time, you'll adjust, it's been a long journey, you've got a touch of exhaustion."

"Intergalactic dissonance, you called it."

"Oh, you heard that, excellent. Yes, I think in the old days, before hypersonic transports, I think they called it jet lag. You cross enough time zones, your body and your mind get out of phase, confused about time, location, sleep, all that. You'll adjust, give it another day, you'll see."

"Another day…"

"Yeah, sweetie, you've been sleeping like the dead for a

good twelve hours. But that's local time. For you, it's more like 27 hours, give or take. But you look great, and the pajamas fit perfect."

I looked down at my body, naked save for a skimpy bit of cloth, not much larger than the 'sleeping suit' from my stasis pod. "Pajamas, that's what you call this?"

Freddy started laughing, then leaned down and kissed me, our second kiss in centuries. He held his lips near mine and whispered, "It's all I had that fit you, and I know you don't like sleeping in the buff. Ergo, pajamas."

I started to laugh. It started as a chuckle, then it veered toward something maniacal, then back to a chuckle as Freddy gripped my hand.

"Help me up," I said.

We walked to the glass wall, where I stared in awe at the beauty and grandeur splayed out below us.

A lone ray of white light emanated from the lighthouse at the far end, the very final end, of the cape. The beam swept over the dunes, over the marsh, caressed our tinted glass, then continued along its arc.

Freddy wrapped his arm around my waist, pulled me close, looked down at me and asked again, "What do you think? Is it everything you dreamed of?"

I looked up at Freddy, then out at the marsh again, and the harbor in the distance. I glanced around the room, then back outside. I didn't know how to answer him. How could I? I didn't know if it was real, a dream, if I was alive, if I was dead. Was I still in my pod, drifting through space? Was I really there, in that improbable place I knew, but had never visited? Or had I? There was only one thing I could do.

I looked up at Freddy, forced a smile, and said, "Do that thing, you know I like it, that thing you learned in London."

"Not London," he corrected, correctly, "Paris."

He reached down, ran his hand over my right butt cheek,

then grasped it in a way that involved a strange contortion of his hand and fingers, a way that should have hurt but instead sent shockwaves of pleasure through my body.

He continued squeezing and said, "You mean this?"

I turned to him, fell against his body, "Yes," I said, "exactly this."

He took his hand from my backside, wrapped his arms around me, "Welcome home Jonny, I love you," he said, and I was certain he meant it.

What I was not certain of, and I'm still uncertain, was whether any of it was real, or something else, something *both unreal and my reality*. But after he pinched me, I thought, 'If I have to rate the *probability* of this *being* real, based on my training and experience, I'll go with about 62%.'

And if a guy like me tells you there's a 62% chance a beautiful world such as this is real, you take those odds.

And never look back.

Stars

He was the unlikeliest of rockstars. No producer believed in him. He didn't look the part, tall and gangly, a mop of early-grey hair, a face that seldom smiled.

But when he played his guitar, people paid attention. It was a beautiful instrument, a '36 Martin D-45, acquired second hand at what was nevertheless an extraordinary price. He mortgaged his future against its strings, but over time, his appreciation of the instrument's beauty was rewarded.

He had friends he believed in, and they believed in him. Together they formed a band, a band that changed everything. He wrote heartfelt ballads and soaring anthems. They toured the world until the band's name became known far and wide. Until their success became too great a burden for their friendship, and their bonds began to fray.

The drummer lost his way in a forest of bad decisions, wasting his wealth on vices easy for a poor kid from the sticks to pick up when the money piled high.

The keyboardist lost interest; his voice was never heard. He knew how much better they could be if only they'd listen.

The bassist felt disposable. It ate at him until his soul digested his spirit and all that remained was jealousy and anger.

The rhythm guitarist, bored to indifference, wanted to burn it all down. He found beauty in destruction, the implosion of a high-rise.

On the eve of what would become the band's last performance, the guitar, the rockstar's talisman, went missing. He had other guitars, of course, but the Martin might as well have been his right hand. He'd put so much into it, had gotten so much from it, its absence filled his life with emptiness and anguish.

Accusations flew, threats were made, and the audience went home angry and unfulfilled. The keyboardist gave his ultimatum, the rhythm guitarist kept his silence, the drummer had a drink, and the bass player made a confession. The guitar was gone, he told them, destroyed in a fit of jealous rage.

They went their separate ways for years. Over time their animus grew, even as their fame faded , and their songs were lost to time. It didn't take long, in the grand scheme of things.

The rockstar found a kind of peace, laced with sorrow and regret, different from the life he thought he'd have, the antithesis of stardom.

He landed in a home near a cliff overlooking the northern sea, embraced by dark winters and cold isolation. He met his wife and started a family. He wrote music he thought would never be played, words never sung. Then, on a birthday like the others he never celebrated, the boys in the band, seasoned by the years, arrived with an opportunity for forgiveness he could not ignore.

It was the drummer's doing, long after sobriety had taken hold. He knew the bassist had lied, all those years ago, when he found the rockstar's guitar in the window of a thrift shop. The instrument showed its age, mistreated by lesser musicians who knew nothing of its provenance, or its power. The bandmates arrived together at the house atop the cliff, their gift wrapped in a simple cotton cloth.

Though it couldn't be played, the rockstar wept when they handed him the instrument. He knew it was his the moment he touched it. He embraced the faded wood, missing frets, broken steel strings hanging down like tattered cobwebs in the corner of an ancient ruin. He clutched its neck like a long-lost lover.

The rockstar placed the beaten relic on a stand in the

corner for safekeeping, walked back into his room made for music, his old friends following, and took a seat on a low stool. Instruments sat akimbo, longing for someone to bring order to their chaos, to make use of their ivory, wood and brass, strings of gut and steel. Reunited once more, the bandmates settled in, and began to play.

They wrote nothing, made no recording, earned no money, acquired nothing material from their efforts, yet gained everything they were lacking. Their reunion expunged the pain of their collective absence, and revealed once more the reason they'd joined together in the first place. They'd found their way back to their brotherhood, a family once again.

Year after year, after that day, they gathered in the small room and played whatever they wanted, filling it with music, and remembering all they'd done, or failed to do, together.

Once they'd all passed from this life to the next, their children would do as they had done, gathering in the room, choosing the things they held most dear, making music for everyone and no one.

The old guitar, restored to its former glory, held in its place of honor, began again to fade away. The rockstar had kept it close at hand, to cradle and strum in those soft-lit hours at the end of life. Then he set it down one last time. Its luster faded, the depth of its meaning lost on the next generation.

Decades passed, then on a birthday celebrated like all the others, a great-grandchild of the rockstar spied the guitar in its corner, near forgotten. She was drawn to its aging beauty, compelled to touch it, at first gingerly, a light stroke of a single finger. A tone soft as velvet came forth, filling her senses. She caressed the fine twisted steel of its strings and heard another note that pleased her. Encourage and enthralled by the beauty of the sound, she strummed a few chords, and sang a simple song, unaware generations of her family, ancestors who lived in the music, had been drawn from their rest by the sound to witness her beginning.

Some would say she was born to be a star, she truly looked the part.

She had a quick smile, a finespun voice, and a family history of music and love and overcoming. She grew to play the guitar as a bird's wings grow to play the air.

Before long, her friends, cousins of a sort, followed suit, each taking up an instrument to complement the other, and they formed a band.

A band that would change everything. Not with stadiums filled with adoring fans, but with music and words filled with the power born of history and fate, love and forgiveness. The guitar carried her forward, elevated her artistry, and the spirits of the departed that dwelled in the music bore witness to it all, and waited with infinite patience for the next reunion.

My Favorite Part

You barely trusted me to drive you out to the frozen pond, deep in the forest owned by my family. You held my gift, the box large on your lap, not wrapped but bound tight with a blue ribbon.

At the frozen shore, on the bench my grandfather made for his young bride, you opened the box and laughed. You lifted one skate, then the other, and announced, your words making clouds close enough for me to breathe, "I don't know how to ice skate, are you planning to teach me?"

"If you'll let me."

"Is the ice thick enough?"

"I came yesterday to make sure."

"All planned out, you're an enterprising man."

"I know what I want, I'm willing to work for it."

"You've got your work cut out today," you said, and kicked off your boots to change, "Help me with the laces?"

"Sure," and I did, then retrieved my own pair from the truck.

You were a glorious disaster, at first. It was my favorite part, the grip of your strong hands, holding onto me to keep from falling, which you did anyway. I didn't mind falling with you.

Then a miracle, you found your legs, and our laughter became cotton-clouds of joy, trailing behind us as we circled.

Then you fell on your backside again, and I swooped in to help you up. Instead you held my hand, pulled me closer. That was when we shared our first fearless kiss, fearless of being seen, discovered, exposed. I fell onto the ice and melted into you, you into me, until I couldn't breathe without you. I knew then what we had was real, could last, if we could keep it. My family, your job, all the pressure *not to be* who we knew we were. Pressed to be unhappy in roles we didn't want to play.

Your beard left tiny ice bits clinging to mine, some of me migrating to you. I brushed the bits away. You laughed so loud, for a moment I fell back into fear. Then my laughter joined yours, remembering we were safe there, in the midst of winter's desolation.

Years from then, decades gone, we return. And now, the land ours, the life less hidden, friends to join us, warm drinks and fellowship. Thin hair turned grey, beards shaved away with the years of our youth. And yet, by some strange magic I've grown older than you. What secret do you hold, to preserve such youth?

You help me with my laces, lay your hand on my knee, look into my eyes. My crows feet spring from the corners with my smile.

"Do you remember when…"

I interrupt as I often do, "How could I forget?"

You help me onto the ice, our friends already sweeping about, graceful and free. You take my hand, hold me steady against a fall, your gentle grip, my favorite part.

About the Book

As a kid, my school library fed me a steady diet of the best science fiction of the day. Authors like Clarke, Heinlein, and Asimov went home with me every week, carrying me to places I could hardly imagine. Television shows like The Twilight Zone and The Outer Limits deepened my love of speculative storytelling, a passion that continues to this day.

The stories in *Pax Liminalis* are an homage to that literary lineage, shaped by the expansive imagination of those early authors and the philosophical sensibilities of Rod Serling and his contemporaries. These stories explore transformation, boundary-crossings, and existential questions.

Influenced by the satirical science fiction of Kurt Vonnegut and Douglas Adams and the soft dystopian vision of Philip K. Dick, *Pax Liminalis* inhabits the space between satire and sorrow, science fiction and social commentary, the absurd and the deeply human.

It is a collection of speculative and literary stories that explore the fragile territory between who we are and who we become — stories about finding peace at the edge of change, calm in moments of transition, and the enduring human search for identity.

About the Author

Ronald McGuire writes stories about change—how it arrives, how it reshapes us, and what remains in its wake. Blending literary and speculative elements, his fiction explores identity, memory, and the moments that define and redefine who we are.

He is the author of the novels *Beyond Tomorrow's Sun* and *Beyond the Rivers of Time*. *Pax Liminalis* is his second collection of short fiction, following *Nightmares & Lullabies*.

Ronald's work spans fiction, essays, journalism, and scriptwriting, with publication credits including Flash Fiction Magazine, Drunk Monkeys, The Dead Mule School of Southern Literature, Winning Writers, and CNN.com.

Learn more at ronaldmcguire.com or beachbookpress.com.